I was teleported into a magical reality that transcended time and space. *The Soul's Journey* is a delightful, thought-provoking, educational, inspiring, and endearing narrative that engages the body, mind, heart, and soul. Good storytelling is an art—one that Warren King has mastered. This is indeed a story that will change the world. I was spellbound.

> — *Cathryn Taylor, author of*
> The Inner Child Workbook *and*
> Which Lifetime Is This Anyway?

The Soul's Journey covers many subjects we need to know to enrich our understanding of God's grand design and to discover our path and mission—and it's written as a lively adventure, which makes it a fun read. Warren covers many areas of health and healing drawing from his practice in holistic health and Oriental Medicine. He shares with us an array of practical wisdom as he describes the necessary preparations of a soul prior to birth, illuminating aspects of karma and reincarnation. In a comic manner, we learn how entities and demons can disturb our lives. In grand overviews, the story spans from Earth's past, back to Atlantis and Lemuria, into our future progress enabled by greater spiritual aware-ness. Out of the thousands of spiritual and health books available today, this one stands out.

> —*C. David Lundberg, Author of*
> Unifying Truths of the World Religions

This story deeply touched my soul. Through the eyes of Narayan, I got an awakening glimpse at how we live and learn in the heaven world between embodiments. Warren illustrates the types of physical, mental, emotional, and spiritual challenges we all face on Earth. Our choices will either help or obstruct us in fulfilling the mission we promised to complete in this life. Touching on the wisdom of many great teachers through the ages, this engaging book unlocks our inner memories and reminds us that we have heavenly friends waiting to help us. All we need to do is ask!

> — *Bradley C. Davis, CEO,*
> *Mercury Learning Systems LLC*

Once you begin reading *The Soul's Journey*, you won't want to put it down. Warren takes us gently and entertainingly through dimensions of being usually inaccessible to our outer understanding. Reading it, you may tune in to details of your own soul's journey—as I did! Moreover, Warren skillfully integrates the fruits of his 25 years of practice in the healing arts with stories and illustrations that outline key elements of diet, lifestyle and energy. It illuminates life's karmic components, relationship dynamics, and more. Anyone reading it will gain understandings vital to their self-mastery and happiness, and the fulfillment of their destiny. A gem of a book—I love it!

> —*Kathie García, Astrologer and Author of*
> The Hero's Journey Through the Zodiac:
> Sun Signs

The Soul's Journey

A Prelife Adventure

Warren King

Lynne,

May your joy so shine
to those you love that earth
may become heaven.

Love,

Lanto Press

The Soul's Journey
A Prelife Adventure
Warren King

Copyright © 2018 by Warren King and Lanto Press

Print ISBN: 978-1-7321612-0-7
Library of Congress Control Number: 2018904827

Published by LANTO PRESS
15612 Highway 7, Suite 252
Minnetonka, Minnesota 55345

Printed in the United States of America

Cover art by Marius Michael-George
Editing & layout by Denis Ouellette

More information, addition copies and formats at <u>WarrenKing.com</u>

~ ~ ~ *DEDICATION* ~ ~ ~

This book is dedicated to all the children who have come from higher octaves of Light and who have been carefully prepared to enter the density of this physical plane with all their dreams and vision intact, that they may play their role on the screen of life and help to usher in such a Golden Age of Wisdom and Joy that the world has never seen.

May their masters, angels, and guides protect and direct them from above. May wise parents, teachers and friends enfold them in love and keep them healthy and happy, that they may outpicture their divine plan and stay attuned always to the voice of the inner self—The Great I AM.

There is no greater power in heaven
or earth than unconditional love.
The nature of the God force at the center
of both the spiritual and physical planes
is best described as pure
unconditional love.

—WAYNE DYER

Joy is the serious business of heaven.

—C. S. LEWIS

It is better to conquer yourself
than to win a thousand battles.
Then the victory is yours.
It cannot be taken from you,
not by angels or demons,
heaven or hell.

—BUDDHA

Books have always been my friends and have assisted me mightily on my quest on the spiritual path. As a child, I was stimulated beyond consensus reality with *A Wrinkle in Time*. As a young teen, my mind was broadened by JRR Tolkein's books on Middle Earth. At 16, I read about existentialism and consciousness, then received an even deeper understanding by reading Carl Jung. At 17, after reading *Siddhartha* by Hermann Hesse, I knew I wanted to become a buddha—an enlightened being. I read *Be Here Now* by Baba Ram Dass and then took out all books from the local library I could find on meditation and taught myself how to meditate. At 19, I read *Autobiography of a Yogi* by Paramahansa Yogananda and learned about walking the path of the Eastern Adepts. At 20, I read the Hindu Sanskrit scripture *The Bhagavad Gita*. I also read *Unveiled Mysteries* by Godfre Ray King and learned about the Ascended Masters and the heavenly beings who, throughout the ages, have worked through different avenues to bring the teachings of Heaven to our dimension.

At 21, I started going to the quarterly conferences held by the Summit Lighthouse. There I experienced hundreds of live dictations by the Ascended Masters through their messenger at that time, Elizabeth Clare Prophet. Since the time of Godfre in the 1930s there have been several such trained and attuned people that could accurately bring down the messages higher realms. Not only was the wisdom of heaven imparted, but also was transmitted to us the tangible presence of the light and power of the higher levels of spiritual reality.

We humans love our stories. Although I have read dozens of spiritual books, I always felt that it was when the teachings were giving in story form that they were most impactful and memorable. Science shows we are 22 times more likely to remember a story than a fact. I started writing this book about ten years ago but then put it on the shelf and focused on my work as a practitioner of Oriental Medicine and holistic health. Now after 25 years in practice, having seen at least ten thousand patients, and with my kids all grown, it was time to dust this book off and polish it up it for release to the public.

I hope that you can imagine that you were once in heaven preparing for this life. May you tune into your own agreements, vows and intentions that you made before you came down here, fulfill your reasons for being and then assist in the birthing of this new Golden Age that is now dawning.

— *Warren King*

~ ~ ~ *A C K N O W L E D G E M E N T S* ~ ~ ~

I would like to thank Denis Ouellette, lifelong friend and fellow chela on the path, for his expertise in editing and typesetting this book, not only for his technical skills, but also for his deep understanding of the spiritual teachings and nuances in this book. I am deeply grateful to my son Lars, and to Nancy Kolze and Alice Sydow for their additional edits, which helped us put the final polish on the gem.

Thanks to Connie Kroskin for the illustrations used in this and my earlier book, Love Your Organs, Love Yourself. Thanks also to Nancy Kolze for her proofing skills and to all the others who read this and gave valuable feedback.

I want to give credit to my wife, Paivi, for being patient with me when my head has been in the clouds all these years as I have downloaded all this information.

My gratitude to my children, Lars and Amanda, for teaching me how to welcome souls from higher dimensions into this world, how to assist in their gestation and birth, how to educate them, feed them, heal them, guide them and then set them free.

I am especially grateful to all the Masters, Elohim, guides, archangels, angels, and elementals who have helped me on the inner levels. Their overshadowing presence has been vitally important in helping me find my calling, my health, and my happiness.

May I never forget to be grateful to my own Divine Self, my Mighty I Am Presence, who has allowed me to come down to this level of Earth so that I could fulfill my Divine Plan and move forward towards achieving Oneness and my Ascension in the Light.

~ ~ ~ PROLOGUE ~ ~ ~

The stream sang and bubbled its way through the flower meadow, falling in cataracts and then flowing under the stone bridge near the white gleaming marble buildings. It was at this exact spot that Narayan stood what must have been many decades ago during the first moments after his arrival. He contemplated the structures that reminded him of ancient Greece, with various pillars and domed buildings perfectly arranged to promote maximum harmony.

He felt a movement behind him and was amazed to see a deer gently approaching. He put his hand out as deer came up and nuzzled him as he stroked the gentle creature that bent down to drink from the stream. "There must not be any hunters in these parts, I've never seen such a trusting wild animal," he thought.

Then he saw a group of four youths approach and sit down among the flowers. They sang as they pleated the colorful flowers into one girl's golden locks. She flung her head back and started laughing, and then they all laughed as the girl started to rise from the ground while seated. He blinked and she was on the ground again. He stood up and he beckoned the girl to approach from the other side of the bridge. But instead she chose to walk across the stream, but she didn't sink into the water, but stayed on its surface. That is when it struck him: "I am really dead!" The tunnel, the light—it wasn't a dream; this is really happening.

Now he looked back on all of the experiences he had. He had been here for so long, yet it was still like a flash. It was so comfortable and enjoyable. There was never any discord to cloud his days, it seemed that this experience would never end. That is when it hit him. "I've been dead for what on Earth must have been for several decades!"

There is not the sense of time here as on earth. He was totally happy here, all his wishes were being fulfilled, but lately, he felt a longing to be back in the fray of time and space and difficulties and density, tears and hope. It didn't make any sense to him— things here are so perfect—but the desire to return was getting stronger and stronger and could no longer be denied. It was time to meet with his teacher and guide and start making plans. It was time to incarnate yet again.

CHAPTER 1

Trying on the Garments

"**W**ell, Narayan, are you ready to make the preparations for your descent?"

"As ready as I've ever been... which has never seemed enough."

"It has never been for lack of preparation, but failure to apply and remember everything you already know."

"Yes, Baltar, that is easier to say now, but it has been quite a few centuries since you've set foot in one of those monkey suits..."

"*Hmm...*"

"I know, I know. I am grateful for the opportunity to prove the highest ideals in the densest realms of God's Mater, the Earthly kingdom."

"Better... and as far as what you'll be wearing, now is the time to try on your new duds."

"Oh, this part! It always feels so tight, no matter how large a model I get! I wish I could feel as light and free as I do now, even when incarnated."

"As a pure unclothed soul, what can you do to affect anything down there? No one can see you, hear you, or even feel your thoughts or feelings. You have to vibrate through something in order to register to even the subtlest senses of the embodied ones."

"I know the need. I'm just expressing how it feels... simply suffocating."

"It's not that bad, and you have all the tools of consciousness expansion you've been studying in order to take refuge in the reality you feel on this side. Besides, it is quite temporary—even the oldest ones all say that it was all over in a flash when the end comes."

"Yes, the illusion of time... to the newly embodied ones it makes no sense, but soon they are indoctrinated into it until they become prisoners of it."

"There are many thousands of souls depending on you to fulfill your mission. Are you going to stick to the plan this time?"

"I will! I know I'm not in this alone, and with help from friends like you, I promise, beloved teacher, I shall not fail this time!"

"Hold my hand, my child, and I shall safely transfer your soul from the radiant garment you have been wearing. This robe has enabled you to experience the frequencies of the Heaven realms. Now, wrapped in my own forcefield, you may inspect this divine clothing in greater detail. Without this garment you would be in the formless realms of pure ideation—a place, if you can call it that, where you would not feel comfortable at your present state of evolution."

"O Baltar, it is beautiful... so white and glistening, so flowing..."

"You have worked hard on these stitchings. It is embroidered from all your positive and divine experiences, thoughts, meditations, and kind actions. In this etheric body of pure and holy light, you have all these memories, woven into this magnificent seamless garment, that you will need in order to recall all of your inner experience here— all your plans, your ideals, your purposes and your mission."

"Surely I will be always happy and healthy when embraced by such wondrous elegant beauty."

"And so it would be, for in the flow of scintillating energy of this body of spiritual fire, there can be no illness or discomfort of any kind, for life flowing in these perfect patterns would suffer no decay or blockages of the life force at all. For all who dwell in the cities of light, vibrating at these high frequencies in the realms of sky above this dear planet, which the inspired of Earth refer to as Heaven wear etheric bodies such as this, and suffer none of the limitations that seem so rampant in the lower realms—even though all were once given such unsullied garments when they too first descended."

"Is that why the bodies and eyes of the infant seem to have an inner glow and such a joyous sense of vitality and pure life?"

"So it is, and so shall it be for you. If your light is allowed to flow freely into your newly formed physical body, never will that sense of boundless energy and joy be diminished, and never would so-called disease or even death touch you unless you willed it so."

"And, I suppose, the second garment I wear shall tell me why this state does not last for we who descend into the veils of time and space?"

"*Ahh,* in my aura, you can read my thoughts, for behold your next vehicle of golden light!"

"How interesting and detailed the design is—and yet, it seems to be two garments in one. The outer one is more brilliant, as a shining sun, but the inner part seems somewhat flawed, with certain dark areas and missing threads."

"My son, it was you who wove also this body of mind. The higher mental body is singing with all your best thoughts and ideas, visions and concepts. The lower mental body, which is quite useful in its own way for logical conclusions and mechanical thoughts, can hardly be called inspired. The dark areas and missing threads represent the karmic patterns that could not be totally transmuted by your meticulous work here, for you have woven much in your last round below. Prejudice, negativity, doubt and illusions have darkened or even severed the delicate mental silk that could have been kept pure."

"Alas, I fear what this might portend for me, and I will diligently work at reweaving these flaws, for I recall what drudgery it can be to have an uninspired mind when in those lesser realms."

"Are you ready to view the next garment, which is most challenging to master for the masses of humanity, yet whose destiny it is to have under total conscious dominion?"

"I am. I enjoy a good challenge. You recall I was fond of taming wild horses five centuries past on the plains of Mongolia."

"You would think that it is as easy as teaching a dog to eat meat compared to the challenges ahead of you, for this is the third of your lower bodies, this body of *e-motion*, or *energy-in-motion*. The mastery of the emotions is one of the main reasons why people take incarnation. It is when you are in embodiment that you can rub elbows with all sorts of people and can be put in so many situations where you must learn to be loving and harmonious. We will put many stumbling blocks before you in your next life. They are but tests for you to be happy and at peace in the midst of crisis. You see, the emotional body is not one you have developed to any great extent, in a positive way, in many of your most recent exploits."

"But it looks fine to me, nice and pink and soft...

"Look closer."

"Oh, yes! What are those hardened dark objects, like seeds? Some are as tiny as strawberry seeds, others larger than walnuts."

"Ah, my astute one, not by accident have you likened those to seeds. For, you see, in the folds of this, your astral body, are the seeds of all your untoward desires, as well as those desires that tended to benefit your evolution. The soft pink covering was a gift to allow you a good start in life buffering the seeds with a tender love for you as a young one, but when conditions are right, the corresponding seeds will unfold. Some will seem as the whisper of a breeze of a mood, others will manifest as a storm to be weathered for months on end."

"Baltar, that brings up a question in my mind that has been a conundrum for many. Is it the environment or the innate qualities of the soul that determine what one becomes? As they say, is it nature or nurture?"

"*Ahhh,* a very pertinent question! But one for which we have tried to leave very big hints. On Earth, one has just to look up and see the answer that is right there."

"You mean, to God?"

"Yes, but in this case, I also mean the luminaries, such as the sun that you orbit, and the solitary satellite that encircles you, the moon. Do you think that it was just an accident that the moon, which is a million times less in mass and diameter and so much closer than the brilliant orb, your home star Sol, happens to be exactly the same size when viewed from Earth, as plainly seen during a total solar eclipse?"

"So are you saying that the sun, which represents the self or inner *nature*, from the perspective of Earthly life, appears to be equal in power and importance to the moon, which is the nurture aspect of our environment, and can overshadow our nature in determining our development?"

"This is why I chose you as my student! You grasp quickly the nature of things."

"It is your teaching that unfolds my inner knowing, beloved guru."

"That reminds me, Narayan, here is a gift that I have

reserved for your journey... it is valuable beyond measure. Guard it well and it will serve you well."

"It looks like a crystalline ruby heart!"

"Yes! It is the jewel of the heart. I place it carefully in your heart lotus, that you may always sense with the inner heart of that central chakra and see things as they are, through the lens of love... This will enable the union of your inner heart with the three upper chakras, and especially your third eye. For if you continue to see only with the two-eyed vision, I can see your mission will again not be complete. But with every gift comes responsibility. If you fail to use it, you may lose it, and thus lose much."

"How do I use this gracious gift, dearest teacher?"

"Let us consider this emotional body before you. Look at any of the dark seeds, and then look again through the jewel of the heart and feel what it tells you. It will not be a logical thought, or a linear message, but an instantaneous knowing. It will not speak twice. When you know, trust... then act."

"Sounds mysterious, like when you were the abbot of the Zen monastery in Japan those hundreds of years ago. I didn't always get your riddles then, and I wish I understood clearly now."

"Pick a seed, any seed. Look and see!"

"I will pick that mustard-seed sized one and if I have faith as of that size, I'm sure I will see with my heart.

"What is your first thought? Out with it."

"It is the tendency to get highly irritated if I am falsely accused of something."

"*Aha!* I knew you could do it, my boy!"

"Yes, but isn't there also a positive side of righteous indignation?"

"Indeed, there is, but the key is in this emotional body and your complete mastery over it. It is one thing to state the truth, succinctly and with power and authority, and proclaim thy true innocence; it is completely another matter to send out waves of anger and discord, resentment and blame, poisoning not only your own aura, but also those about you. Have faith in the Law of

Universal Justice. And know that the light shines in the darkness and darkness comprehends it not, but tries to snuff it out. You are and are destined to be, the Light of the World—even as you are the Salt of the Earth!"

"I suppose I have to brush up on my Bible studies to keep up with your messages, but I think I understand the heart of the matter."

"Why don't you try a somewhat larger seed? And fear not, because since you are not yet in embodiment, wearing that emotional body, you can watch it in a somewhat detached manner and not be swept up in the waves of feeling. This too is good practice, for while on Earth, you still can examine your garments objectively through introspection and meditation, and thus root out these noxious weeds that would sprout under the proper circumstances and stifle the flowering of your garden of happiness."

"I choose that large oval one, there."

"What do you see? Again, only with your heart, and the first impression you receive. That will be the correct one."

"It is quite complex, but I will try to describe it. It is the tendency, fed over long eons of time by my own life force in great repetition, to be so obsessed with my mission and work as to almost totally ignore my other responsibilities, mainly the happiness of my spouse and offspring."

"Again, well done. I have great hope that this gift of heart perception will help you immensely in finishing up what we call *the mighty work of the ages*. You must remember the dual purpose of this venture. Not only is there the main mission as your unique gift to lay on the altar of humanity as service, which in the teachings of India, we have referred to as dharma or divine plan, but also there are your personal debts to life— your sins if you will, either of commission or omission, which according to the Great Law of Life, you must pay back if you would graduate from Earth's schoolroom and permanently move on to the Higher Road of Life that we walk here. This is termed *the balancing of your karma.*

Karma simply means action. For even the first law of physics on Earth tells all that for every action there is a reaction of equal force—thus negative karma must be balanced."

"So am I fated to suffer in turn all that I have imposed upon others as suffering?"

"In general, yes, but forget not that the happiness, also, that you imparted will come back to roost in your branches—tenfold."

"Is there no way to mitigate this law—this eye-for-an-eye, tooth-for-tooth self-imposed judgment?"

"It is a complex matter. Motive plays a great role in the laws of karma. Someone who harms another by accident has accountability that is far less than that which is carried out with premeditated maliciousness. But the scales have many ways to find balance. We have found that the piling up of debts that many have made is so grievous that it would take exceedingly long spirals of time to balance them, and thus, many would simply give up when seeing the ponderous road of tears that lies before them."

"So, there is another way?"

"Yes, my son. There is grace and there is mercy. The Master Jesus, when in the flesh, did reveal much to the masses on the Law of Forgiveness and he made clear that faith was key, but also that faith without works was dead. And so good works, service, sacrifice, prayer, selflessness, and certainly forgiveness of others... these are like money in the bank in payment of one's karmic debts. When the debt comes due, by the Law of Cycles, these *funds* may be used to mitigate, and sometimes entirely eliminate, the debt accrued. The key is to forget the self—as the Master said, *"Those who lose their life shall gain it."*

"Oh, that gives me great hope!"

"Indeed it should. And forget not that revealing these great truths to those who are ready to hear them is a mighty way to blot out mountains of heavy karma. For thereby, you can greatly assist them in the process of balancing their own debts and ensuring that they do not further engage in the creation of more entangling karmic webs."

"Great master, is there no way of eliminating these seeds, that they might be impotent in their ability to even sprout?"

"Your questions are well chosen. May you always so question until you have found out the answers to life. There is much you can do about these seeds. I recommend to you the hobby of gardening in order to understand this subject at a deeper level, for all on Earth has been given as symbol to the soul in her upward progress, and the book of Nature is open to those who have the eyes to see."

"Well, I know that unless the soil be fertile, nothing will grow."

"And so it is with these, thy many tendencies, called *samskaras* in Sanskrit. In gardening, the sprouting and seedling stage is the most delicate and will determine in which way the plant will grow and the quality and quantity of the desired fruit. In human life, it is the period from conception until the age of seven that will greatly influence which qualities will become permanent habits of body, mind and feeling—and which ones will be snuffed out for lack of nutrition, if you will."

"It seems almost unfair that so much power should lay in those few years and in the hands of one's environment and caretakers, who most often know little, if anything, of the gardening and caretaking of the body, mind and emotions, let alone the soul."

"Indeed, it seems so, but it is none but yourself who chooses your environment, as well as your parents, based on your *karma*, your *dharma* and the *samskaras*, as we have been discussing. We must deal with the great ignorance of this present time, and sadly many of our best plans have yet to manifest due to the dense burdens under which this planet dwells. Many of our best souls have been distorted so badly in their vehicles, whether through illness, sometimes inadvertently made worse by well-meaning doctors, or through other psychological distortions, that their earthly missions as a whole remain unfulfilled. Nowadays many are prevented from even entering the realms of action at all. There are many who glibly insist on their freedom of choice, and while free will is the law of Earth, there is yet no freedom from the responsibilities that radiate from the use of that same will."

"And are there other ways, besides the soil quality, to impede the unfolding of these ancient karmic seeds?"

"Again, the answer is yes. You can successfully sprout the beneficial seeds of positive qualities first, which will naturally repel any of the more negative weeds from taking root, even when they become awakened by circumstance."

"Is there no way to just destroy the ability of a seed from sprouting at all?"

"There is, but it is rarely employed. It involves the use of fire, spiritual fire, to heat up the bad seeds and destroy them and their potency. This involves a one-pointed focus on the things of the spirit, deep and profound meditation, intense prayer and the ability to let the light of your higher etheric body and even your higher bodies to shine forth through you. This embodiment of light will not only be for your benefit, but also for the world as well."

"I see how important the emotional body is, and its mastery. I will give it due attention so that my mission not be curtailed for lack of development there."

"You are becoming wise. Even the Earth tells of the importance of the emotional element. Of the four elements, water is just one, but it covers three fourths of the surface of the planet, and constitutes the same proportion within the physical body itself. And of all the waters on Earth, perhaps a mere one percent of it is in a form usable by man for his nurturing. It is this fresh water alone that is a veritable deep symbol of the Love of the Divine Mother that nurtures all seeds. So it is love and love alone that can ensure that your best seeds thrive and that the garden of your soul is bountiful and vibrant."

"So if water is the symbol of this emotional body, then the air would be the mental body, and fire the spiritual body?"

"Verily, it is so, and your reading of scripture will make more sense if you recall this symbology."

"And the fourth element?"

"Very well, then let us proceed to the final form—the one that all will see and judge you by, but is in essence, the shadow of who you are—your body of earth."

"Pray tell, dear teacher, how can you show it to me here when it shall be formed in the womb of my mother?"

"I shall show thee. This here is the prototype, if you will, upon which the physical body shall be precipitated. It looks like a replica of your form, but is what is referred to as the etheric double—your lower etheric or fire body."

"Is this what I will look like in my next embodiment? Couldn't it be made, a little more... *ummm...* handsome?"

"Do you want to be accepted and loved for who you are, or for your most temporary of forms? Besides, your physical appearance has been governed by your own karmic choices and propensities. For instance, a weak jaw indicates a tendency toward a weak will and the enlarged nose... how shall I say, a bit of an enlarged sense of self? Anything else?"

"*Umm...* What are those rivulets of energy flowing up and down?"

"Those are what the Chinese have termed jing-luo or meridians of *chi*— your life force energy. In India, they would say it is circulation of *prana* in the *nadis*. The rules are simple. Keep them flowing smoothly and evenly and you will enjoy perfect youth and health. Block them up, overflow them or reverse their direction, and you will enjoy these no longer."

"And what, may I ask, would cause me to do such a foolish thing?"

"Asking is simple, Narayan. Answering is not so easy, but I shall try. First, let us assemble the four lower bodies one inside the other. These can be likened to the *matryoshka*, wooden Russian nesting dolls. You will notice how these differently vibrating envelopes partially interpenetrate each other. Upon further close examination, you can see that there are spiral points where the energy from the higher etheric light body can flow through the mental and emotional matrices, into the lower etheric, revivifying and directing its flow and vitality. These are the points that are used in the practice of acupuncture."

"Okay, what do I do now?"

"Touch the pink portion of the aura at the level of the emotional sheath, right on the rather large seed corresponding to your liver under your right torso... Yes, that one. Now let us imagine a scenario where you are driving a car in bumper-to-bumper traffic."

"This will be fun! I haven't driven since my 1938 Desoto..."

"Focus on the task at hand. You are struck from behind, sustaining minor damage to the rear of your vehicle and the Ferrari behind you has its front end totally caved in. The policewoman arrives—to whom the gentlemen behind the wheel calmly states that *you* must have inadvertently placed your car in reverse and backed up into *him*. When you try to deny it, the driver of the maroon Porsche to his right says that *is indeed* what happened."

"Why, how can those dirty, lying, spoiled, rich..."

"My, my! You are feeling lower emotions for the first time in decades and is that the best you can do? Look at the red energy surging into that peacefully content liver! Look at the meridians down the inside of your legs lock down in stagnation. See the kidney meridian back-flow as you fumble for your insufficient-coverage insurance card and note how the adrenals pump wildly as you pant, sweat, and clench your jaws. I dare say you have just decreased the longevity of your maiden voyage in your new vehicles by about four months. And what did it take... all of four minutes? *Hmm...*"

"Okay, okay. You got me there. I guess I have some heavy cramming to do... When did you say we depart?"

"Well, you may rest for a while and later, we shall review the choice of the fortunate parents and siblings you are to... how shall I say, enjoy?"

"Don't frighten me now. I remember this part from before. You are always so reassuring beforehand, but when I get there, I remember nothing, they remember nothing, and it is like the blind leading the blind."

"*Ahhh,* but you forget your gift so soon—the jewel of the heart. You shall not be blind—you can't be, because too much is riding on this one. You will have help; you only have to ask."

"That is comforting. I hope I remember to at least do that!"

"Affirm victory and it shall be yours. Now, rest in peace and prepare."

"That's very funny. Here I am, having been dead for over fifty years, in constant creative motion, and right before I have to go back into the dream of so-called *life* again, you tell me to rest in peace!"

"Perhaps it is the fulfillment of someone's final prayer for you at your last funeral!"

CHAPTER 2

The Previewing Station

They both laugh heartily together as Narayan puts on his etheric body and goes to a special room charged with the holy vibration of peace by those who serve in preparing souls for their next round of incarnation in matter. No sooner had the idea occurred that he would rather like some refreshment than a goblet of crystal immediately precipitated in front of him, hovering before his gaze, sparkling with effervescent light. As always at this level, whenever a thought or question arose, the answer was immediately forthcoming in his mind. For here, everything is made of consciousness—as is all creation, visible and invisible—but here, beyond time and space, there exists no lag between a desire and its fulfillment.

Immediately he knew that this was a concentrated form of life-energy that would help sustain him through the difficult decisions that lay before him. As soon as the sparkling nectar reached his lips, his entire being tingled with intense joy and bliss. To his astonished happiness an entire tub of this liquid now appeared before him and he needed no prodding to immerse himself.

He hung up his emerald robe, a symbol of the scientists and healers of this retreat. He draped its shimmering golden sash above it, indicative of the wisdom that he had realized in passing his initiations with his beloved teacher. As he settled into the sparkling, revivifying, fiery liquid, he felt closer to the source of life than he had since his travels soon after his initial passing from the screen of life, those five decades ago.

For, you see, his own grandmother, who was a source of

strength for him throughout his life, now permanently occupies these rarefied heights. Here he had no right to tarry; neither was it entirely comfortable for him to do so. It was she alone who spoke to him as a boy of the glory of the things of the Spirit and the emptiness of the illusions of Earth. She told him of the mystical paths trod by the founders of all of the world's spiritual traditions, and a few of their followers. She warned him to judge no one, but to focus on the oneness of all. *God is Love and God is One, and the true self of you is one with that One*, she was fond of saying. Not all the adults thought she was so wise. Some thought her fanatical in her focus on the things of the Spirit. It seems that those who are judged to be less on Earth, are often the greatest in Heaven.

She passed when he was just twelve, but since that time, whenever he was at a crossroads in life, he just thought of *Ule' Nanna* and was given enough comfort and strength to make the right and the tough decisions. So, it was no wonder to him that it was she who first greeted him upon his passing. Graciously, she allowed him to relax in her luxurious and fragrant garden while he tried to make sense of all that had recently transpired.

It was only now, as he lay in this bath of crystalline liquid light contemplating that experience, that he realized that the garden he so relished, was entirely created out of her mind with all the comforts, which she knew would give him peace—even down to the smallest detail, such as the gooseberries he loved to pick when he visited her farm at the turn of the century.

As a pleasant tone sang its comforting pitch through the room, the dimmed space became brighter, although from no apparent source of illumination. Narayan arose and robed himself and this time was hardly surprised when the entire room instantaneously vanished and an attendant appeared and without a word directed him to the previewing station. Narayan wondered what the life of this monk-like being was like. How interesting it must be to be able to see all the plans, hopes and dreams of incarnating souls and then compare this to what actually takes place.

Then his thoughts darkened for a moment—perhaps it is

sad, for how many souls actually remember and act on their memories in the frequently difficult atmosphere of time and space? How patient they must be to be able to watch so many who abdicate their highest ideals, for money, comfort, doubt or fear, and then totally ignore the ministration of the multitudes of spiritual beings that try to draw their attention back to their original divine plan.

With one deep glance from his guide, Narayan quickly reassembled his aura, which at this level is as plain to others as it is to oneself, and assumed his customary positive expectation of success. For he had been well taught that expectation, whether conscious or unconscious, is the same as prayer and indeed often more powerful. For prayer can be done with the mind alone, but expectation is faith—coupled with e-motion and visualization—that something will indeed come to pass. Yet still, many are surprised when their worst fears come upon them. Thus well is it written: *Pray as if thou hath received it already.*

Then this thought came into his mind, as if whispered to him by his teacher: *Divine direction is available to everyone on Earth. There is a path that has been laid out for everyone. Fixing the attention on the Presence Within is the key to contacting the higher levels. Faith in God is one thing, but trust that you can tune in to its Divine Direction is another. Just because you have a plan is not the guarantee of its success.*

They paused at the door, and just as Narayan's composure was completely regained and his will steeled, the door swung open to receive them. He was ready for any images to be portrayed on the great living screen. He was ensconced in the faith that these great beings that were about to aid him had only the highest intentions for his soul and were in cooperation with the will of his Highest Self. Their work was now to develop the most beneficial script possible for his accelerated evolution and service to the planet.

"Welcome, beloved soul!" It was a beautiful female master along with his teacher Baltar who was also rising at her side.

Baltar introduced his companion, "Narayan, this is Renatia, an ancient master with a special knack for assisting incarnating souls to make the most of their next round on Earth. Lately I have been calling her in to help my students with the previewing process prior to their birth."

"Well, Renatia, it is my pleasure to meet you," Narayan joked, "but for an ancient master, you don't look a day over twenty-four!"

Renatia replied, "All glory to the Light of God, sir. And it is my pleasure to meet you as well, as I have a particular interest in the mission that you are about to fulfill."

"I am pleased that you are so sure of my success. But if you don't mind, may I ask a personal question?"

"Feel free!"

"How is it that you became a counselor to those of us who are about to incarnate? What are the prerequisites for such a position?"

"Well, not too many of my pupils have queried into my own history, but I will tell you. Sometimes failure is the best teacher and the best impetus for achievement. I had three lifetimes in a row where I came back to my own teacher and soul group with a mark of failure on my file—failure to achieve my mission. I can tell you, I cried burning tears of remorse. How could I have allowed paltry sensual pleasures and their constant seeking of gratification to make me utterly forget my purpose, my reason for being? My friend, only when you have fallen down for the last time, can you get up and say, as a solemn vow to yourself, *I will not be fooled again!*

"From then on, in my final earthly embodiment, I studied hard, I took every course, read every book, and sought out every expert in the field of time management, success, and reaching one's goals. Since then I have been setting and achieving my goals, until now I am privileged to help others in achieving theirs."

Narayan paused, considered what she had said, and replied, "Thank you. I now have even more trust in you. I am now ready for my preview, and I wish to balance the greatest amount of negative karma as possible."

Baltar replied, somewhat jokingly, "It seems to me I have heard that one before... but even the byways you have chosen, and the sketchy secondary plans we have had to engage, have been instructive to you, and you have learned well what *not* to do!"

Renatia added in a somewhat more positive note, "I think you will do quite well. You have prepared long and hard. Come beside us and let us pray in our hearts for Divine Direction."

After a few minutes of silent prayer, they sat facing the large screen before them, concentrating their attention on Narayan's life to come. The cloudlike radiance began to rotate, coalesce and come into resolution, like the focusing of a telescope. Images appeared, which, although on a screen, were more experienced in the mind and heart. Thus they seemed to be a real experience, including emotional frequencies that would be absent from a mere video screen.

"This is a projection into the home of your prospective parents. They have signaled on the inner that they will accept you. Now they must confirm it on the outer," whispered Renatia.

A woman sat, apparently in great torment, as she repeatedly examined the thin blue line that appeared across the white rectangle embedded in the plastic base of the pen-like object. "Pregnancy test," was Renatia's hushed commentary, "positive two times in a row."

Narayan tried to maintain his composure, but he couldn't help feeling that to start out with one strike against him did not bode well. Sensing his thought, Baltar enveloped him in the comforting presence of a loving father.

"If only those who would be parents would realize that their first moment of discovery that they are expecting a life is often sensed by the would-be soul incarnate. Then should they always rejoice, for the higher realms have chosen them to be the vessel for the descent of great opportunity. For it is not for pleasure or ease that souls descend to the earth-plane—the uncomfortable process of birth should remind them so—but it is for growth and the opportunity for spiritual development, which is abundant on both sides of the equation."

"I'm sure I can get her to love me; she doesn't even know me yet. When the shock wears off, perhaps I can get her to feel my gratitude to her for providing me with the form that I need and that Earth needs in my mission."

Baltar commented, "But she does know you! Once the tables were turned. You were sent to a home for unwed mothers, and you tried your best to care for her, your little baby, giving her what little you had. She never discovered who her father was, and was herself married to someone prematurely who was never able to give her the love she so craved. That husband is now her first son."

"She seems to have a lot of issues with men."

Baltar replied, "It is a misalignment with the masculine aspect of her own soul and her relation to the Father aspect of God. This theme has been repeated for some centuries. Thus, to allow her to focus on this issue, she now has two teenage sons, both conceived when she was just ending her own teen years, and now here, another son is on the way."

"Yet instead of getting the hint, "Renatia commented, taking up the flow of the conversation, "she has become more hardened in her illusion of being a victim of life, of being punished by God, when it was she, in consultation with us, in this very room, who consented and helped construct this very *dream*, which down there they call *life*."

"*Ah,* I can see my father-to-be coming in the door. I have hope that he can be a positive influence in my development."

"Indeed, he will be," Baltar said, in an upbeat tone. "He is a true scientist, for his mind is open. He also has a hobby as a carver of wood, which itself has taught him many of the laws of life. You will have to forgive him for not knowing all the spiritual laws of life as we understand them from our perspective. He will do his best to teach you to be a kind and generous person. We will

attempt to accelerate him spiritually."

"Do you think he will recognize me?"

"It is entirely possible. He is open to the idea of re-embodiment. He has studied the cycles of nature and has seen how all unfolds in a pattern of a spiral."

"Oh, look, she is showing him the pregnancy test. What will be his response?"

For the first time, the robed monk who, as a disciple in training to soon be able to guide souls in the previewing chamber, spoke, "It is my experience, that this is the time to pray and send positive and hopeful expectation. The projection of the sensation of a chill going up the spine and hair standing on end is often a useful one in letting them know that they are in contact with a synchronicity from other dimensions."

"Pregnant! Are you sure? I thought we were beyond, I mean... *Ohhh*, that is quite strange—odd indeed!"

"What do you mean, strange?"

"Oh, no, not you dear. I mean, when I was speaking, I felt a tingling sensation run up my back and over my skin, and I thought I heard... Oh, no, that's not possible."

"You heard what?"

"A voice, but not a voice—more like a thought in my mind."

"Well, what did it say?"

Chokingly and with a tear gliding down his cheek, he sputtered, "It said, *I love you, Daddy.*"

As the couple embraced, a cheer resounded in a grateful chamber somewhere in another dimension, separate and yet exceedingly close to the happenings of the little home on Earth.

"What about my brothers? Can I view them also?"

Renatia breathed deeply and then said tenderly, "You may have had enough for one session. You see, Narayan, much has changed in the culture..."

"I'm ready now. Are they in trouble of some kind?" Narayan asked.

Renatia continued, "They are quite normal for this day and age. They are 12- and 15-year-olds in a technological age. They are named Aiden and Roger, respectively. Watch the screen... We will condense four hours into a few minutes..."

"Wow, everything is technology these days! They are plugged into electronics for four hours straight."

Renatia commented, "The wires hanging from their ears are connected to what's called an iPod, or maybe it is their cell-phone. I have a hard time keeping up with all this technology. Amazing, isn't it? Thousands of songs contained in something so small."

"But that ruckus I hear is just noise!"

"That is not how they hear it. They used to call it rock-and-roll. I'm not sure what they call it now, there are so many new genres."

"What are those murder games showing on the TV?"

Baltar answers, "That is what I think is called a PlayStation 2. It is an interactive video game. Mostly they are pretending to murder and gain power over their enemies."

Renatia interjected, "This is as old as play itself. In the old days, they would play cops-and-robbers, or cowboys-and-indians, or toy soldiers, or Risk or Monopoly."

Baltar continues, "The sad difference here is the intensity of the violence, and the video component robs them of their creative powers—the ability to create one's own visualization and thought forms. Here they passively take in someone else's images. The question is will they be able to truly create on their own when the time comes?"

Narayan asked, "What about the half-hour TV show? What was a 12-year-old doing watching a show that was mostly about sexual relationships?"

Renatia answered, "The chakras below the heart are being overstimulated by all these programs. And of the half-hour, about twelve minutes consisted of commercials.

Baltar commented, "And what do they advertise but drugs to stimulate sexuality to people that are so drained of vitality that their bodies cannot function normally on their own? The rest of the commercials are mostly for other TV shows depicting affairs, sexual innuendo and violence."

Narayan queried, "What was that rectangle that Roger kept pulling out of his pocket."

Renatia commented, "That is the new craze, cellphones. People used to talk on them, now they also type messages back and forth, called *texting*. There is nothing wrong with being connected to friends, but for many virtual contact has become a substitute for genuine connection. Facebook is another way to while away too many hours. It can be rather, how would I say, excessive."

Baltar responded, "There is lots of communicating of surface information, but there is less deep communication of the deep feelings of the heart and spirit. And it is good to enjoy some moments of silence in the day for one to commune with the inner self and the higher mind."

Renatia added, "Notice the etheric body that surrounds the physical. It is a bit diffused and grayish; that is the depleting of the reserves due to the constant bombardment of electromagnetic fields."

Narayan chimed in, "In the old days we used to spend hours a day outside, sometimes playing pretty rough, but we had a lot of vitality and hardly any child was ever sick with a cold or obese."

Baltar asked Narayan, "So what do you think of our choice for your incarnation?"

"Well, I think I'll be able to balance out all the technology with some good old fashioned fun, but I'm concerned about the lack of spirituality. What if I start to forget everything I learned up here? Have you checked other possible families that still have purity and with which I have karmic ties?"

Indeed we have, Renatia answered, "Finding a spiritual family in the West is increasingly difficult and the wait is long. There were some in the poorer countries, and we considered India and South America, but your karmic ties lie mostly in North America and there your education can be accelerated, especially if we can influence your father to begin instructing you early on."

"So what about these brothers of mine? If they are in my family I must have some karma with them, right?"

Baltar quoted, "It is written, *your enemies shall be of your own household.* This is both literal and figurative—allegorically it indicates that all your negative thoughts and feelings that are suppressed shall still dwell in thy temple, and literally it means in terms of reembodying with those you have ties to, even in the same family. And hatred or non-forgiveness can often create a stronger bond than love. This is why forgiveness is the only road to freedom from those who have wronged thee."

Renatia took up the idea, "It is like gemstones in the rough; when they are placed in great proximity and rubbed together they become smooth and radiant—*the rough places are made plain.*"

Baltar then spoke along the same vein, "Even in our retreats we often put together the souls who have had the greatest discord between them and assign them group work. Finally, when they learn to function harmoniously together, they graduate and can join the soul group with which they have a more natural affinity. They are invariably grateful for the experience in the end. Of course, this is somewhat easier here than in the dense physical body where all memory of the purpose of life is often hidden from the conscious mind."

"So these brothers were my enemies?"

Renatia explained, "Actually, they were, should we say, confused. You were the abbot of their monastery in Europe in the 1600s. They looked up to you and followed your direction in their prayers, meditations and disciplines. But then you started to have your own inner mystical experiences and direct revelations from the Spirit. You started to doubt certain doctrines that you had previously preached—such as sin being the common state of all men merely because they are born in the flesh—and you publicly doubted that God would consider us sinners merely because the first ancestor Adam had made a mistake. You started to preach that we are all Sons of God, not only Jesus, and you found plenty of Bible quotes to back it up."

Baltar concluded, "It was only a matter of time before the higher ups in the Church hierarchy heard of your blasphemies and it was these two souls, your future brothers, that testified against you at an ecumenical hearing, often exaggerating in their testimony against you."

Narayan exclaimed, "I can remember it now. They accused me of preaching the doctrine of re-embodiment. In my defense I quoted some early Church Fathers and even the New Testament itself."

Baltar interrupted, "Your recall is correct. Needless to say, the Holy Spirit revealed all of this to you, but this fact did not budge their prejudice in the least. All they could say to refute you was, 'If you quote the likes of Origen of Alexandria, who was a heretic and whose writings are anathema, then you must be a heretic as well."

Renatia continues, "Consider yourself lucky that you were not tortured or flogged, but defrocked as a priest and banished from the city. You lived out your days in great holiness, but also great poverty and loneliness, and you could never totally forgive your students for betraying you. Thus you forged a tie with them, which has waited all these centuries until you could again come back and work it out through love and forgiveness."

Baltar confirmed, "We have seen it again and again. There is no injustice anywhere in the universe, in the long run."

"Well, I certainly hold no ill will against these two souls."

Renatia praised his attitude, "That will bode well for you. We have waited until your ages are separate enough so they will not pick on you, and you won't engage in the usual sibling rivalry. Because of their misuse of energy in attacking others, their quotient of life-energy has been diminished this time around, and their unfortunate addiction to soda has exacerbated their adrenal decline, along with the long hours in front of the TV and computer. In other words, they have little energy left to make more karma with."

"You consider addiction to soda serious? That affects nearly half the people on Earth!"

Baltar spoke gravely, "We consider it quite an imperilment, especially to the youth, as it is a threefold poison. First, there is the great quantity of sugar, about 8 to 10 teaspoons per can, but masked due to the carbonation in liquid form. Sugar is a sinister soul poison, as its intensely expansive nature, called *yin* in Chinese medicine, weakens not only the fibers of the physical body, but also the integrity of the finer bodies, enabling the precious energies descending into the temple from on high to be spilled or siphoned off by dark entities. The intestines and brain become lax and judgment becomes fuzzy. Sugar, due to its impairment of judgment and quick thinking, has caused many more accidents than alcohol ever has. Hardly any that regularly partake of it in large quantities can be a true disciple, for in effect, it is nearly impossible to discipline the four lower bodies under its influence. Secondarily, there is the caffeine content."

Narayan interrupted, "Well, if coffee is another devil, there goes the other half of humanity."

"*Ah hum!* As I was saying, cocaine was the drug of choice used by the original soda companies, as in Coca-Cola or Pepsi. When this was made illegal and the soda fountains were about to disappear, the manufacturers resorted to their second-choice stimulant, caffeine. Thus while some adults get their coffee made decaf, which it really is not anyway, the manufacturers pour the excess caffeine into artificially colored sugar water for the children, ensuring another generation of addicts. The effect on the adrenal glands from constant overstimulation, along with the fears of daily life, amplified by the media and video games, ages these children so quickly that they are old in their finer bodies before they have even started to mature.

The third attack is through the carbonation in the water itself. You see, plants take in carbon dioxide and release oxygen, the physical counterpart to *prana* itself. People take in the oxygen and expel the spent carbon dioxide. When taking in this waste product, carbonic acid is formed in the blood, which not only weakens the bones, but also acidifies the entire system.

Renatia added, "When the bodily fluids become acidic, rather than a healthy alkaline in pH, there is the open door to all known infections and inflammation."

"Hopefully, I'll remember enough of this to stick with water!"

Renatia commented, "I hope so. Unfortunately, your mother to be is addicted to the so-called *Diet* version of soda that has become popular since your last descent. It contains a deadly combination of two seemingly harmless amino acids. But this aspartame is in a class of compounds called *excitotoxins*, as is the chemical MSG. These excite the neurons of the brain to fire so rapidly that they begin to die. Since its inception, there has been a steep rise in brain tumors, migraines and epilepsy. And the amazing thing is nobody has ever lost weight by drinking the concoction—it merely makes people desire more sweets and so they actually gain weight.

"Well, if this is true, can't the scientists just expose these facts to the public?"

We have inspired Earthly scientists to discover that artificial sweeteners throw off the balance of the good bacteria, which leads to weight gain."

"So why don't you expose all these attacks on the bodies of the people to the scientists and to the public?"

"Oh, my child, are you still so innocent after all these lives! They put fluoride, one of the major carcinogens, as well as chlorine, which after combining with organic matter in the water, forms serious poisons, into all their drinking water. They even sell water for babies that is doused with these poisons. Does anyone seem alarmed that their toothpaste tube states plainly on the label: *Call Poison Control if swallowed?*"

"What child doesn't swallow toothpaste?"

"Exactly! And when we send our best minds into their midst to sound the alarm, they are conveniently fired, silenced and threatened. If they are too outspoken, they are sometimes even killed. It is like this in every area of life. Just try to sound the dangers of microwaved food, electromagnetic fields, genetic engineering, excessive and imperfect vaccinations, and you can have your initiation of the crucifixion right here in the twenty-first century.

Narayan thought for some time and said, "I hope you are sending many more than just me. This seems like an all-out battle for the future of civilization and life itself on planet Earth!"

Baltar replied, "The great masters, of whom I myself am a humble student, have a grand plan for a wonderful golden age of enlightenment and freedom. They have carefully crafted their plans and sent well-trained and courageous souls into the fray to awaken the people. The established powers and their control over the government and media will try to oppose this, but the people, many of whom come to our retreats in the higher realms while their bodies sleep at night, are rapidly being awakened. But don't underestimate the dark forces...

"We are at a crossroads. Dark ones are in control of many of the major corporations and are in high places in government. The business of modern medicine itself has not been illumined by true wisdom. Greed and the profit motive are corrupting influences at every level of business and government. The same companies that run the businesses that are killing people become the heads of government agencies that are supposed to limit their power. We do not blame all doctors, lawyers, or government workers, but so few have remembered their inner vows and their high purposes. However, enough have succeeded in fulfilling their missions that the people are starting to wake up."

"Yes, there is hope." Renatia continued, "You can see this in the growing popularity of natural and organic foods and of so-called *alternative medicine*, which is, in reality, the way that God has created health and balance though the agency of the Divine Mother, through Nature herself."

Narayan added, "I know people down there think we are just sitting on clouds up here playing harps, but as St. Thérèse of Lisieux said, *I want to spend my Heaven doing good works on Earth.*"

Baltar, putting his hand on the shoulder of his pupil, enveloped him in a hug of light, a peach light circling him around with the fragrance of a rose. "My son, we are truly of one mind and heart. It is this desire that binds us together in service forever—for we are on *the path of the bodhisattva*. That is, we sacrifice even our own complete happiness and bliss in the eternal oneness in the Light in order to maintain a part of ourselves as separate individualities down here. We thus extend a helping hand to those trapped below in the veils of illusion."

"Do you mean that they don't have the wherewithal to contact the etheric planes of light on their own? Unless those like us volunteer, they would have no way to make it home to our Father/Mother God?"

"In the main, this is true. Occasionally a soul will have enough fuel in her rocket to transcend the levels of earthly density, but these are few and far between. And we need souls like you who still wear your karma on your shirtsleeves, so to speak, who can take on bodily form and rub elbows with those still trapped in illusion. And because you have suffered, as most of us have, in order to get where we are, you have developed compassion. That selfless love will be the magnet that will draw others to the same path that we trod.

"For if we, as masters ascended, were to appear to them in all our glory, the souls below would praise our greatness at first, and yet look upon themselves and their mistakes with such shame that they would sooner sink back into the night of their unconsciousness than face their own self-creations with eyes open and choose to walk the path of redemption, resurrection and ascension. And thus the great proliferation of drugs and all manner of activities that lead the soul away from matters of the spirit, through the senses and back into the outer world.

"Wait... I just received a projected thoughtform from a master who ascended five hundred years ago after numerous heroic lives in the country of Japan. He has chosen to maintain somewhat of a Japanese appearance when visiting these etheric levels, for he has attained to great heights through his one-pointed zeal and stupendous discipline and attainment. He was a favorite abbot of a major Zen monastery in his last embodiment, famous for his exquisite sense of humor. And thus he calls himself Gomasio, which means *sesame salt,* for he has made it his focus to bring his Eastern art and science of diet to the Western world. Although he knows the highest heavens and the realms of nirvana, he chooses to focus on the body and its health, a subject which he feels is the key to liberation for millions of souls."

CHAPTER 3

Master Gomasio & the 5 Elements

There was a heightening of the energy vibration in the room and all went into silent meditation as a shimmering, cylindrical beam of light began appearing in their midst. Slowly the form of a robed, seated master appeared to float within it, about four feet from the floor. The outline was slowly filled in until he appeared to those in the room as completely tangible, much as they were to each other. The main difference was that he remained floating in the lotus position and that the dancing, shimmering, radiant beams in pastel shades of light emanating from him were deeper and more intense than Narayan had ever seen before.

The group bowed before him in the Japanese fashion and he addressed them with a slight Eastern accent. "I could not help but overhear your conversation and felt led to come to you to give this blessed soul a teaching that will assist him greatly on his forthcoming journey into the shadowlands."

Narayan addressed the master tentatively, "Master, how did you know I needed your instruction at that moment? Why would you come from such lofty heights to instruct a neophyte like me?" All the while, he wondered why this inscrutable being seemed so familiar and dear to him.

"*Ahhh,* dear Lo Han, or Narayan as you are now called, there are no secrets in Heaven, for all is made of one mind. We who have unified our being with the cosmic mind exist in a realm that is beyond all appearance and form, no matter how subtle. We can *hear* all frequencies that resonate with our purpose. It is like a spider who can feel every silky strand of her grand web and quickly navigate to any area, without ever getting stuck herself."

"Although, in this case," Baltar exclaimed, "instead of being a fly for your dinner, we are the receivers of your great blessing and outpouring of wisdom, beloved Goma!"

All laughed heartily. Narayan began to wonder at the strange sensation he felt when he was addressed as Lo Han. A pulsing sensation, almost like the rhythmic opening of a flower bud, was activating in the back of his etheric brain.

Sensing his query, Gomasio explained, "Ahhh, Lo Han, you have forgotten. We have been together thrice before in a very close way. Once you were my fellow samurai, where we cleansed a village of ruffians; once you were my disciple in a Zen monastery... and still now you ask many questions; once you were my beloved son, Lo Han, when you became a great healer, as you followed me on my rounds and inherited my clinic, *Circle of Jade Bamboo*, after I passed on.

Suddenly a flood of emotion inundated the soul of Narayan and the memories washed over him and all that was spoken of was recalled in great detail and clarity. This is the wonder of the etheric plane, where the Akashic Records of past lives can be so easily accessed. Gomasio then stepped lightly to the floor and the two embraced as a loving father and son who have endured long separation. Baltar, Renatia and the guide who had escorted him hence, bowed silently and slowly disappeared. When Narayan again opened his eyes, he was amazed to find himself in a magnificent yet simple Japanese garden. Peacocks and swans, herons and colorful birds unknown to the mankind of Earth strutted happily amidst the delicately carved hedges and fragrant flowers. A veritable rainbow of fish splashed contentedly in the ponds, which seemed to radiate an almost audible sense of peace.

Goma motioned for Narayan to be seated on the floating lotus-shaped cushion beside him. "This is my retreat, Lo Han. I thought you would enjoy a break from that viewing chamber. Please relax and absorb this important—and I hope exciting—

teaching on spiritual nutrition. It is here that I teach those who are being instrumental in transforming the diet and eating habits of the West, whose pernicious habits have even tainted the East, and thus lay the foundation for the great age of enlightenment that will soon be dawning on that blessed orb you call Earth."

"But Goma, with all the great spiritual teachings and great wisdom that you can impart, why would you focus on food, which is so... basic?"

"*Ahhh,* you will recall that all those who spread the dharma, the teaching of the Buddha, to the people, had first to become healers. For how do you expect someone to contact his inner self when their outer mind is completely engrossed in the pain, inflammation, and irritations of an ailing physical body, as well as the ensuing distractions in the feeling and mental bodies? The physical body is the base of the pagoda—if there be termites and a faulty foundation, all shall collapse in a heap."

Goma paused, and in answer to mental call, which never failed to surprise Narayan, two disciples, one male and one female, appeared to either side of them and poured them each a cup of tea and left a small ball on the plate beside it. After a slight bow, they vanished.

"But, Master, you came to us when Baltar was about to explain the danger of drugs in drawing awareness away from the inner reality. What has this to do with food and diet?

"Many on Earth consider themselves above the taking of drugs, for they would not inhale and inject substances to alter the chemistry of their brains. Yet all that is partaken of becomes part of the body and brain; it influences perception and thinking and thus the soul's spiritual awareness and evolution."

"So, are you saying they are addicted to food? Everyone has to eat or they will starve."

"All life is a process of taking in, and giving out. Even in the higher dimensions, we absorb, assimilate and eliminate. But for the angels, their food may be light, love, devotion and prayer. Certain initiates and adepts can transmute vibration into substance. There are the many records of saints living for years on merely the energy contained in the consecrated wafer of Communion of the Lord. Yogis have subsisted merely on the prana contained in the air and water. But for most, food is given as the precipitated love of the Divine Mother for her children in form, the distilled essence of sunlight into plants, and thus it should be regarded. And all have the choice of what they put in their mouths, and by this exercise of free will they can control their destiny.

"Yes, Goma, even children will teach their parents of this choice of food from the very beginning, what they will or will not put in their mouths. The rest they will smear on the floor, or on their clothes or the walls!"

"Well noted, yet the choice offered to the children in these modern times, even in the womb, is of such poor quality that many a soul's mission has been delayed or even entirely aborted as a result of either the physical diseases, or emotional and mental distortions arising from their poor diets. And the drug-like nature of certain foods naturally leads one to seek the ever-increasing stimulation of the nervous system and glands, first through the socially acceptable addictions to caffeine, chocolate and refined sugar, or onto the many illegal forms of sensory stimulation."

"Are you also saying that the soda and sweets that the great majority of mankind partake of is a step toward drug addiction?"

"No, not at all... it *is* a drug addiction. They will tell you that it is just the taste or smell that they like, but if you have them stop for three days, then they will understand the withdrawal symptoms of an alcoholic or heroin addict. You see, all drugs have receptors in the brain and the central nervous system that elicit certain feelings. The body itself can make these molecules by itself, for instance, soothing painkillers or relaxing endorphins when one gets injured. One may even train the body to produce these substances through meditation and biofeedback. But the primary reason the chemistry is thrown off in the first place is through the daily diet—in addition to overstimulation and stressful thinking and feeling."

"Master, you are going too fast; this is all so new to me! I have loved a cup of coffee in the morning as much as everyone else, and always had a stash of chocolate in my drawer, but never considered my spiritual evolution to be hampered. I thought that food was food and spirit was spirit."

Goma retorted, "Everything in moderation, Lo Han! It is not: *Eat, drink and be merry, for tomorrow we die!* Or how about, You only live once! How shocked they are when they find out they must pay for every jot and tittle, as it is written. What different choices would be made if they were to say: *Eat, drink and be merry, for tomorrow we will live forever*? The truth is that most foods are not good or bad for everyone. For many people, coffee can be quite beneficial, and dark chocolate has a positive effect for many as well. For others, it may be their downfall and a harmful addiction."

"Goma, please tell me more about the effects of food and diet on spiritual development, as well as health."

"This is a large subject, but it can most easily be understood by the two basic forces of the Universe that the one eternal energy first manifests as. In the East, this one balanced force is called the *Tao*. It may be called the Law or Will of God as well. It acts impersonally, like the law of gravity. The *Tao* is divided equally into the two forces of *yin* and *yang*. *Yin* is an outward, expanding, centrifugal force. *Yang* is an inward, contracting, and centripetal force. Examine anything in existence and you can see that any object or activity has a preponderance of one or the other. Traditionally, the *yin* expanding force has been described as feminine while the *yang* contracting force is seen as more masculine...

"We see all of nature manifesting in a balance of these polarities: north and south, positive and negative, light and dark, hot and cold, etc. But to better explain the staggering display of the detail of creation, the two forces are seen as flowing into each other. When you have breathed in all you can, you have no choice but to exhale, so *yin*, at its extreme, flows into *yang*, and vice versa."

"Oh, is that why the *yin/yang* sign has a little white in the black fish, and a little black in the white fish, all in a circle?" asked Narayan.

"Very perceptive. Since the *Tao* is one, they can never be completely separated, even men have female hormones, and women have male hormones, it is the preponderance of one or the other that will determine the so-called masculinity or femininity in a given individual. Now, as the *yin* turns to *yang*, there are five basic stages that the energy passes through."

"Are those related to the five elements described in Eastern medicine or the four humors described by some ancient Western physicians?"

"*Ahhh,* you are remembering some of your past lives! For you have used these principles in many cultures as a healer and a scientist. Allow me to demonstrate this process."

Goma rubbed his hands together and slowly separated them with palms facing each other. As he sounded the *OM*, a distinctive, pulsating energy could be clearly seen between them— a bluish energy emanating from the right and a pinkish hue from the left. As the two forces collided, they began to spin in a circular motion forming the ancient pattern of the *Tai Chi*, rapidly revolving but seeming to only move in a slow clockwise circle. As he again chanted the *OM*, but in a much higher pitch, the pattern took a quantum leap into the form of a pentagram, an upward pointing five-pointed star.

When the star appeared, Narayan immediately thought that these must be the five elements of oriental philosophy. Because deep concentration was needed to demonstrate this teaching in a more visual way, Goma dispensed with the necessity of speech and resorted to his accustomed way of teaching, which was by way of telepathy and the unfolding of thoughtforms in the mind of his students. By taking those he instructed into his own mind, he could have them experience any idea, concept or experience he had within himself in a very direct way.

Narayan looked with total absorption as images emanated from the points of the star, they formed a sort of ring or wheel in which the images flowed one into another with no clear boundary between them. From the top emitted the image of a red, fiery flame, but not just a physical fire, with its characteristic heat and light, but the energy behind what is called fire on Earth. It was pulsating and alive, seeking to expand its boundaries and consume all available. It was an exuberant, buzzing energy. As he put his total attention into this fire, seeking to feel its true essence, he heard an exciting, intense, fast-paced musical masterpiece. With even deeper concentration and one-pointed meditation, he heard the most beautiful voice singing in his heart...

I am the fire of the Central Sun,
The light of life, of everyone,
The heat that keeps the bloodstream warm,
The lightning of the thunderstorm.
Wisdom of the sage's mind,
All impure I shall refine:
Bees buzzing on a summer day,
Children jumping as they play,
Quasars, pulsars, electrons too—
All that's old I shall renew.

The fire that comforts every home
I breathe in every centrosome.
The glint in every warrior's eye,
The faith that martyrs never die,
The glow of cosmos, the light of space,
The speed of thought, the desire to race
Beyond all form and every name.
Behold, I beat thine own heart flame!

As the last note trumpeted, seemingly resounding throughout all creation and bathing it in a ruby light, Narayan lost all sense of his own limited individuality and merged in ecstatic bliss with all fiery energy everywhere. Beyond all limitation in form, he had the awareness of every sun in every galaxy, in all the multiverses beyond time. He felt the heart of all living creatures, from the highest angels, to the lowliest worms, and felt their striving to be one with the source of that light. Expanding happiness engulfed him as he felt he would explode in an uncontainable cosmic smile. Gradually, he became aware only of the flame within his heart and realized that through that light, he had contacted all this fire of life, seemingly *out there* but ultimately within.

Again he gazed, with new vigor and vitality flowing through him, at the blazing pentagram floating before his gaze, held between the palms of his master. The fire imperceptibly merged into the image at the end of the next point of the star. It seemed as if the fire had produced a fine ash that was condensing into soft, rich, fragrant earth. As he thought that this must be the next element, a correcting thought emerged in his mind. The essence of it was that the term *element* was too discrete a conception. All in the cycles of life is a flow of cosmic energies, and thus may be called the *five phases* or *five transformations of energy.* The one life diverges into the polarity of two. In the flowing of one changing into the other through this circuit, five phases may be discerned for the understanding of man, although in reality the gradations are infinite.

Narayan focused on this second phase of energy that some call *earth*—although perhaps *soil* would be a more apt description. He saw how fecund with the potential for life it was, for the glow of fire still ensouled it. He anticipated that a song would begin again but instead, to his great delight, he sensed a symphony of fragrances...

The acrid scent of compost pile,
The diaper of a newborn child,

Earth just turned in garden bed,
The roses of the newlywed,
The freshest air when storm has passed,
The fragrance of the fresh-cut grass.

Then, within this awareness as of a *cosmic nostril*, he could again hear the singing of a gentle poem, as tender as a mother caressing her child to sleep...

I bring the fire to life to form,
Your soul with flesh I do adorn.
Between the seasons I give you rest.
Truly I am the cosmic breast.
I would not have you burn your lips,
You must have reality in tiny sips.
A handful of dirt that teems with life,
If you like, I am spirit's wife.
In volcanic ash new life shall creep.
Pollen sprouting in pistil's deep.
The softness of each petal rare,
Floral fragrance distilled with care.
My joy to serve, as farmers toil,
All you need springs from my soil.

A golden-yellow light filled his soul, soft as amber, sweet as honey, as he was one with all soil energy throughout cosmos. He felt the joy of earth in spring as the misting rain softens its seeds. He understood the embrace of all who love in this world of form: the hug of a child on her mother's neck, lovers united after being long apart, and the handshake of men as they win the game. Earth had transformed into planets as they spun around their suns, some teeming with life, some frozen, some burnt. He could sense that all of life that integrated with this energy had a sense of self, of center, of groundedness and of balance. Those who lacked integration with earth would feel a sense of longing for wholeness as a sadness or neediness, and a greediness for that which can only be found within.

As he again beheld the golden star of life held in balance by Goma, he noticed how that the earth energy was not only on the stellar arm following fire, but was between each phase and in the center of the star itself. It reminded him of the phrase, *between seasons I give you rest*, He intuitivcly felt that this quiescent, maternal energy was the potential energy that gave the turning thrust for the entire circle of creation, and allowed for each phase to flow into the next.

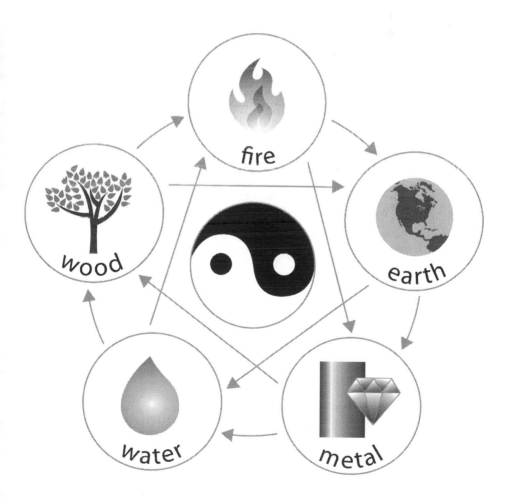

White light began to beam from the third of the five arms. In a strange way, he could sense that the light was somehow thicker, as if there was a feeling of density about it. It was as if the settling energy of soil was condensing into great solidity. Not knowing what to expect, but encouraged by his previous elemental adventures, Narayan again focused his attention fully and relaxed into an absorbent mode.

Still feeling the soft glow of the maternal energies of soil, he was unprepared for the intensity of the message that shot into his mind like a cannon. His entire being tightened. He felt like a solid mass of stone or an iron statue. He sat transfixed as a masculine voice proclaimed:

> *Those on Earth, they call me real.*
> *No phantasm or cloud with me you'll feel.*
> *Hit your thumb with a hammer, bang!*
> *I am the essence that is most yang.*
> *Those of the East, they named me metal;*
> *Perhaps the new age shall call me crystal.*
> *Strength and tension, pressure and strain,*
> *The bone of form, a skull for your brain,*
> *God's kingdom extended to the realms most dense,*
> *Valiant souls, they journey hence.*
> *The fist of the victor, the diamond of will,*
> *The spine of a cactus, an avalanche spill,*
> *To air I am thunder, to water I'm hail.*
> *My iron resists fire, to wood I'm the nail.*
> *To earth I'm the shovel, I'm the essence of men.*
> *The bullet, the sword blade, the tip of the pen,*
> *The teeth of the lion, the nails of a hare,*
> *Feel my power, if indeed you dare!*

Narayan felt himself being thrust downward into the depths of matter. He could sense himself part of all living forms. But this time instead of identifying with the essence that moved the form, he felt the densest part of being. He felt all the rocks and planets of space and felt that they too had life—a sense of being-ness that predated the evolution of self-awareness. He could see how crystals and gems, clear yet hard, focused intangible vibrations into directed energy and useful power. He understood why men need sport and are inclined to competitiveness. He saw how those who were passive and aimed not for the future reached into the mists of the past only to find grief. He felt how gravity pulled all mass to its center. All was still fire, energy and light that condensed itself into this heavy estate. He knew that the purpose of the essence of metal was to bring the Kingdom of God to Earth as it is in Heaven.

He could not maintain this state any longer; the focalized pressure was too much to stand. As he gazed again at the glowing star, it was as if the heat of the depths melted solid stone into molten lava, then cooled and softened. A relaxing bluish energy then began to circulate through his tightened being and he breathed a sigh of relief. A gentle, feminine voice, as a babbling brook, sang her fluid song into his inner ear:

After such hard work, enjoy a shower.
Though I am soft, I have no less power.
My drops, through eons, erode the rock.
My nebulous vapor rusts any lock.
I seek all places deep and low.
I don't run nor jump; I relax and flow
I am the moist eyes of every daughter.
To life I am mother; they know me as water.
Lakes and oceans, rainstorm and dew,
After the drought, all life I renew.
Steam me, I'll condense, freeze me, I'll melt.
I'm the flow of emotion; can't be known, just felt.
I clean out all toxins, remove all debris.
No one can live a moment without me.
Hear me in song, in the cry of the loon.
Poets depict me as the face of the moon.
Restrict my expression and soon you'll be old.

Life is for flowing; water you can't hold.
I love to dance in fountain and spring.
In each beating heart, in each cell do I sing.
My essence can fill the deepest hole.
Feel now my presence, thou precious soul.

A great swell, as of a tidal wave, reared up before him. Before he could even fear, the voice said in a comforting tone: *Fear is for those who know me not, until you have mastered me, it is your lot.* This brought back the painful memory of the next emotional body that Narayan would have to wear in his next Earthy excursion. The wave stood there in powerful, restrained stillness as he reasoned with himself: These archetypes are the essences behind all manifestation, above and below. If he could develop a benign relationship with them now, through this inner initiation with his master, how much smoother and more joyous would be his evolution in this incarnation. With these thoughts he resolved to surrender all fear and let this universal catalyst wash over his soul.

At that moment, the wave let go and he was inundated in a tsunami of bliss. He felt as if he was one bubble in an ocean of consciousness. He let the shell of his individuality burst and the joy of this surrender gave him the assurance that he would be his own self again, although never again entirely separate from the Allness of Being. For now, the awareness of all the forms of water on all worlds was his to experience: The joyous splash of waterfall, the first breath of an ascending spring, the laugh of a fountain. The patience of the ocean as it beats mountains to dust.

He sensed water's power as it doused fires and reduced chains of bondage into rust. He felt how the waters on Earth suffered greatly through pollution and impurity, yet in her sacred essence, she felt eternally free. Her purpose of giving life to nature may be temporarily curtailed, but through filtration and distillation, with the help of her companion elements, she could regain her purity. All rivers and bloodstreams are carriers of life. What sickness is carried when water is burdened with strife!

Then his inner vision widened and he saw that all emotion and feeling was really water in an uncondensed way. Instead of the joy of the spray, and the peace of the still lake, humanity had polluted the streams of life with hatred, anger, fear and despair. The results they manifested in their outer physical world was a reflection, back upon them, of what they had created by their feelings on the inner realm. Narayan made an inner vow to not add one drop of miscreation to the entire astral sea, but to work to refine it back to its pristine purity. His mind now floated as a drop up from the sea and he was glad to assume his individuality again.

The circle at last was completed as the final arm of the five-pointed star began to glow. As the blue waters sprouted into a pale-emerald green, a joyous, healing, revivifying, wakeful energy ascended within him. His eyes glowed with wonder as he saw stretched before him the essence of spring emerging from the sleep of winter. All life stirred and strove upward toward the sun. A voice, as of a youth in his prime, sang sublimely in its rhyme:

The essence of a sprouting grain,
Call me wood or tree—it's just a name.
An upward rising energy,
I am the ascending of the chi.
Grass, flowers, and the mighty oak,
I'm the power behind all growth.
Though I'm the essence of all humor,
When blocked I just might grow a tumor.
Present at spring, I give rebirth,
Behind all laughter, I am mirth.
Upward and onward, my motto and song,
I sing of what's right, not what's wrong.
I wake each bird and every child,
I'm in the wind that runneth wild.
The mist that rises in the morn,
Each new day is the sun reborn.
For all those yearning to be free,
Look within and look to me.

43

Again and for the last time, Narayan was immersed in this, the fifth essence of archetypal substance that supports the drama of matter, called wood but representing so much more. Narayan apprehended the joy of spring, the sprouting of seed, the chicks emerging from their newly cracked eggs, the power that tells the rooster to crow, the geyser to blast, and the rocket to soar. He felt the hope of the dawn and the faith to climb every mountain no matter how high. It was the renewing of all life when seemingly dead. When in tune with this force, you just jump out of bed! When this force is blocked with stuffed anger and feelings unsaid, it turns not to joy but to depression instead.

Now, as with all cycles in life, this intensity of ecstatic experience had run its course. Once again Narayan returned to his normal consciousness and perceived the Master Gomasio standing before him with the five-pointed star. The pupil kneeled and bowed his head to the feet of his teacher. Goma bid him to rise and bow instead to his own God Source, giving glory to the One for this blessed experience.

He said, "You have desired for long centuries to experience the essences behind all manifestation. Through hundreds of lives you have delved, through science and religion, art and philosophy, through medicine and humble service, to find higher truth. Because you have, in the main, used the information and the attendant power behind each veil of nature, to assist your fellow beings, you have earned the right to this experience. Treasure it and remember it, for you have opened a door that shall not be shut and to all its wisdom you shall have access. But woe to any who misuse the attendant powers that come with such knowledge, for the powers inherent in nature and their elemental overseers shall vanquish any who trifle with or misuse these sacred energies."

CHAPTER 4

Experiencing the 5 Elements

"**M**aster Goma," asked Narayan, "how does this knowledge of the five transformations of energy assist one in the realms of Earth?"

"Ahhh, there is much you can study from the sages of the east who have long pondered these mysteries and applied them to human advantage. Perhaps the most recorded is in the studies of medicine and health. There are many texts and charts that correlate each of the five basic elements with many of their manifestations.

"But I'll make it far easier for you, far easier for you to experience and remember than studying a list. He touched the student in his third eye and suddenly Narayan felt the emotion of pure joy, then had the feeling of being outside on a warm summer day."

"Where are we?"

"You are in my thoughtform of the fire element. You are in my mind."

"What? How can someone live in another's mind?"

"Ahhh, you have been in this heavenly realm for all this time and never considered the substance of which it is made. There are cosmic, enlightened, liberated beings that create this entire realm in their mind in deep meditation and by sounding certain syllables of power. They precipitate this level."

"Is this the only level that they manifest?"

"Oh no, every level."

"Even the dense levels of Earth?"

"Different beings create and sustain the physical atoms, the emotional particles, the mental substance, and the spiritual, fiery essence."

"This blows my mind! So we are in the fire element in your mind right now?"

"Feel free to explore."

Narayan bent down and picked up a dandelion plant, chewed on a leaf, and felt the bitter flavor inundate his senses. He looked up at a field of waving corn. A boy stepped out of the field. He could see through him! He saw the fire energy animating his heart and saw his small intestine glowing with a fiery red color. He could make out the network of all his blood vessels. He looked up at the sun at high noon and felt its heat. Then he glanced back at the boy who stuck out his bright red tongue at him.

"Now I can remember studying charts on the elements in the Circle of the Jade Bamboo, but it was nothing like this experience. Now I can never forget the correspondences of the fire element."

"Oh, please, can you provide just such an experience for the other elements, as they are so fresh in my mind? It's as if they are now my friends and I want to know all about them!"

"Friends indeed they are, to those who respect and use their power wisely. Very well, let us experience soil or earth, which is the energy of balance and centeredness.

Suddenly he felt the weather cool a bit, as it was now the Indian summer, the transition towards fall. He approached a golden-pink raspberry and placed it on his tongue and chewed. He felt the sensation of sweetness fill his being—everyone's favorite taste. A woman stepped forth and offered him a bowl of cooked, yellow millet, the grain of the Earth. She had ingested some of it and he could see through her skin, descending into her stomach, spleen and pancreas, glowing with golden-yellow light.

He understood how blood sugar and digestive energy was ruled by this earth energy. It seemed to be afternoon and there was a humid dampness in the air. She flexed her arms to show off her muscles and then blew a kiss. Then, she disappeared and all that remained was a pair of lips.

Then, just as quickly as it began, it ended and he was back with Gomasio. "How does one manifest emotionally in regards to this earth energy?" Narayan queried.

"When earth is channeled correctly, one has a calm, centered, clear, abundant and peaceful energy. But when off-kilter, there is spaciness, fogginess, over-thinking and worry."

"And of the fire, can one have too much joy?"

"Look at the shrieks of one who has won money on a game show or the jackpot at a casino, and the pandemonium expressed by young girls at a pop star concert, and you can appreciate the great strain that this places on the heart. When one is overly dominant in fire, the life of the party they are, but when alone, with no one to shine for, sad indeed grows their countenance, until buoyed up by the attention of others again. A fire cannot burn continually without refueling. In fire, as in all things, balance is always called for."

"Oh, please, continue with the next three!"

"When the expansion of fire settles through earth, it becomes condensed or crystallized into its most contracted state, metal. As Einstein demonstrated in his famous equation, matter is nothing more than condensed energy. All that people perceive as reality is as real as a dream—it is just the close proximity of the electrons and atoms that give the illusion of solidity. Cosmic rays pass through everything on Earth constantly, unimpeded by the relatively vast space between the atoms' particles. From the perspective of these rays, the Earth is completely invisible. In the same way, at our increased vibration, spiritual beings can visit the Earth unseen and undetected, except by those who vibrate at our frequencies. Since all on this etheric plane vibrates at our level, it seems real to us, but to those on Earth, it would seem as a nebulous illusion or dream. Then, when you take incarnation, all your experiences here will seem as a dream, while for us, a lifetime below, even if ninety years long, seems as a brief reverie, for time as well as space are all relative to the frequency of the one experiencing them.

"But I digress. We were speaking of precipitated spirit, or matter, in its most yang and condensed form. Goma held out his fingers and a long, white feather appeared. As Goma moved it along his arm, he could sense his entire skin feeling ticklish. He saw a scene with a beautiful sunset as a middle-aged woman sat under a tree whose leaves were changing to autumn colors, he could sense the life energy being drawn to the roots. She got up and placed a slice of ginger root into his mouth and his whole being sensed its strong, pungent flavor. He could see through her skin and see her lungs and large intestine glowing with white light as the lungs released the spent air and the intestine would be used to let go of the unused refuse of the digested rice she had eaten. She wrinkled her nose at him and then just disappeared.

"So does a balanced metal element let go of the nonessential. Those who hang on to the past may suffer from an *emotional constipation* called unresolved grief. Thus the lungs may discharge these feelings and attachments, as children do so well with sobbing and crying. In the realm of holistic healing, it is noted well that death begins in the stagnation of the colon. Health in the lower torso begins with an active diaphragm and those who do not deeply breathe in the *prana* of life will never attain its vibrancy. It is the infant or child who is told to stop crying who learns early on to suppress their breathing and the discharge of feelings and this blockage opens the door to manifold diseases."

"So, master, you are saying that it is the suppressed negative emotions that correspond to each of these organs that are often the real cause of their dysfunction in the first place?"

"Now you are seeing clearly. If only those on Earth could so perceive. Almost every disease has its seeds in the repression of emotions in early childhood—but there is a circle here, as well. If someone emphasizes the thinking aspect of their mind, and is constantly reading and studying, analyzing and critiquing, worrying and obsessing, without the exercise of the body, or the sharing and expressing through social interaction, a spleen/stomach disorder will likely arise. In addition, if one disobeys the laws of diet through overeating, under-chewing, or poor food combining, then digestive disorders and blood-sugar imbalances shall be created. Over an extended time of such activity, an undisciplined, racing, chattering, unfocused mind will be the norm and insomnia will plague one's nights."

"Oh, to think of the multi-billion-dollar industries that thrive on "treating" the symptoms of the illnesses of body and mind, which are merely the result of disordered eating and repressed emotion!"

"If causes were addressed the entire economies of nations would be so abundant in such short order, and the health and happiness of the population so increased, that criminality would be a strange memory of dark ages, and a time of peace, enlightenment and creativity would manifest, which humanity can hardly even dream of in its present state... And now, the next elemental phase after metal... Do you recall what it is?"

"Well, if the most tightly contracted phase cannot be maintained, as the cycles turn, the energy will flow, horizontally before rising to fire. So first would be water and then the wood."

"Good thinking! You have understood well, Narayan." He slapped his student on the back and suddenly they were transported to a snowy nighttime winter scene with a bent-over, old man trudging through the snow. It was apparent that his bones and joints hurt with each step. Occasionally he would cup his hands over his ears, as he was hard of hearing. Narayan could make out the dark, bluish glow of his kidneys and his bladder.

He could hear Goma saying, "The kidney is the most important in determining the constitution of the body, and thus the health and longevity of the form. Corresponding to night and the season of winter, the kidneys do not like to be cold, although the nighttime and the winter are ideal for healing the tired and stressed adrenal glands, which are ruled also by this energy."

Goma put a large crystal of salt on his tongue and Narayan felt as if he just swallowed the ocean. As he watched the old man shuffling in the cold, Gomasio continued, "The sense organ is the ears and water rules the teeth and bones. In general, old-age symptoms, such as graying of the hair, weakening of the bones, loss of sexual energy and loss of hearing and memory have more to do with the weakening of the kidney *chi* and much less to do with the total number of one's days."

The scene disappeared and Narayan asked, "Are you saying that age doesn't have to do with how old you are?"

"What gets old? The cells are immortal, they replicate and divide and are renewed. Some clever researchers had an experiment in which cells in the lab were constantly fed ideal nutrition and the waste was promptly removed. The cells never aged and unfortunately the project was halted, as the cells outlived the scientists themselves!"

"If only they had experimented on themselves instead of the cells in the test tubes!"

"We all are scientists in the laboratory of our own beings. We all may choose what to partake of, in terms of not only diet, but also in thought and feeling. The process is identical to this experiment in the lab. To the best of our ability, we must take in what is the most pure and beneficial in our environment and eliminate what is toxic waste. In the body, when the elimination organs are functioning well, then even toxins absorbed from the environment, from food, air and the byproducts of biological functions, are effectively discharged. When the cell membranes are fluid and the circulation is smooth, then nutrition is readily absorbed and delivered where needed."

"What happens when the elimination is impeded?"

"The intelligence of the body is amazing. It is able to heal so many conditions. Self-healing is a divine attribute created in every cell of the body. When the Light of the Spirit is in communication with the soul, the etheric blueprint, our original divine design, glows and then can precipitate into the physical—as long as the Light is maintained. Sometimes, this energy can be transferred through the hands of a healer or a person of great faith who can bring about healing."

Master Goma continued, "The etheric double that you have witnessed is the pure creation of spirit and has its own wonderful attributes. The acupuncture meridians are the pathways for the free-flowing energy in this body. In the same way, when one is cut, a scab forms of its own accord. One doesn't have to know how fibrin is created from fibrinogen in blood clotting. It is the Holy Spirit's action that moves through all of life, obeying the laws of creation, which, unlike many earthly laws, are always aligned with Cosmic Law.

"So, let us say that one partakes of foods incompatible with one's body. For example, let's consider the eating of cheese, as it is notorious for being indigestible for many, and constipation results. Waste materials begin to be reabsorbed into the bloodstream and the body will seek a secondary exit. If the kidneys and liver are not functioning up to par, perhaps hampered by fear or anger, as much as by table salt and low-quality oil, then the skin, often called the *third kidney*, may try to do the job. So a skin rash appears, often near the lymphatic tissue, as a means of eliminating the toxic and acidic debris.

"If a suppressive cream, like cortisone, is applied and the toxins are driven back in, then a new route must be found. The lungs have an opening to the surface and so mucous may form and a cough may result. Then again, using the suppressive tactic so prevalent in today's medicine, some antibiotics may be used, wiping out not only the bad, but also the good and necessary flora, the helpful bacteria, throughout the body, especially in the large intestine. Then the real troubles begin."

"Okay now we are ready for this last one, the wood or tree element. He put his hand on Narayan's head and they were in a forest with just the beginnings of bright green leaves sprouting forth. He felt a lemon being squeezed into his mouth and his entire being shuddered with sourness. He felt his gallbladder contract and his liver glow with green energy.

He was back with Goma again, who mentioned, "If you had a marked tendency to sprain your ligaments, if you had allergies in spring, or had irritation in your eyes, you could assume that your liver needs some work."

"This is all so fascinating. I don't think after these direct experiences of the elements that I will ever forget them."

"But for those on Earth, they can always find a chart on the correspondences of the five elements."

At that, Goma held out his hand and a scroll appeared. On it was the chart summarizing the five phases of energy.

"Thank you. Now I am sure I can easily memorize it."

Elements Chart

	Earth	Metal	Water	Wood	Fire
YIN ORGAN	Spleen	Lungs	Kidneys	Liver	Heart
YANG ORGAN	Stomach	Large Intestine	Bladder	Gall Bladder	Small Intestine
BODY PART	Muscles	Skin	Bones and Joints	Tendons and Ligaments	Blood Vessels
COLOR	Yellow	White	Black	Green	Red
FACIAL DIAGNOSIS	Temples, Upper lips	Cheeks, Lower Lip	Below Eyes, Chin	Between Eyebrows	Tip of Nose, Corners of Mouth
MERIDIAN PEAK TIME	7am - 11am	3am - 7am	3pm - 7pm	11pm - 3am	11am - 3pm
ORIFICE	Mouth	Nose	Ears	Eyes	Tongue
PERIOD OF DAY	Afternoon	Sunset	Night	Morning	Mid Day
SEASON	Indian Summer	Fall	Winter	Spring	Summer
SENSE	Taste	Smell	Hearing	Vision	Speech
SPIRIT	Yi / Thought	Po / Corporeal Soul	Zhi / Will	Hun / Ethereal Soul	Shen / Spirit
TASTE	Sweet	Pungent / Hot	Salty	Sour	Bitter
WEATHER	Damp	Dry	Cold	Wind	Heat

© LoveYourOrgans.com

CHAPTER 5

Questioning Germ Theory

N arayan asked, "So, is it not the germs or microbes that are causing disease?" To which Gomasio replied, "When people are catching colds, or even heats, does everyone get sick?"

"No, only a certain number of those exposed."

"There is the key to your answer. Those who do not succumb have a shield. Either the body does not allow the pathogens to enter, or once they do, they find no place to set up shop. These invading organisms love acidic and toxic environments. Nature has a way, through the cycle of life, to break down forms that have spent their usefulness. An accumulation of acidic and toxic debris is their signal to move in and decompose.

Suddenly an image of a grey-bearded man on his deathbed was in front of him. He was weak, but had to speak and in a heavy French accent he said, "It is the terrain!"

"You see, this theoretical debate—*is it the germ or the terrain?*—goes back to the mid-1800s at the beginning of modern medicine with Louis Pasteur's arguments with Antoine Béchamp in favor of the Germ Theory of Disease. Pasteur, the founder of pasteurization, maintained that invading germs caused disease, while Béchamp maintained that germs seek their natural terrain—diseased tissue—rather than being the cause of diseased tissue. Pasteur finally acknowledged the truth of Béchamp's theory and the failure of his own but by then, it was too late. The germ-killing smallpox vaccination had proven to be a moneymaking enterprise and the holistic approach to improving one's over-all pH balance and immune system, and health through nutrition and internal cleansing, would take more than a century to begin to take hold again. The profit-motive takeover of health-care through drugs and vaccines has yet to relinquish its hold on modern medicine."

"So alkalizing the body's fluids and cleansing of toxins would make it so these invading life forms cannot even get a foothold, let alone thrive in an individual."

"Exactly! And the good bacteria are part of the whole defense and digestive systems of the body in the first place. This is why antibiotics should be used so sparingly. So in our example, when the beneficial flora has been drastically reduced through the overuse of antibiotics, the door opens to all other competitors vying for that empty space. There are yeasts, molds and fungi, harmful bacteria, viruses and parasites of innumerable and horrible description that can overwhelm the gut and its ability to fight them off. Once these take firm hold, they are difficult to eliminate without one-pointed effort and a correct understanding. These organisms will eat the nutrition that is meant for the body and will even send out chemical messages to the brain to crave the foods that are their favorites."

"Let me guess... It isn't broccoli and kale."

"Right again. They love whatever feeds their toxic and moldy environment. Sugar is the main fuel for the yeast, along with other refined carbohydrates, such as refined and yeasted white bread. They also thrive on fermentation and will crave vinegar, soy sauce or alcohol. Tomato sauce and potatoes, orange juice and pork will ensure that their acidic nature is well nourished. The chemical preservatives, additives and colors don't benefit them directly, but by paralyzing the immune system, they further their ends of weakening the life force, which would threaten their stronghold in the body."

"Is there any hope once things have gotten so bad?"

"So bad? This is the state of internal affairs of the average citizen of Earth—at least the so-called developed nations who are spreading their practices of poor diet, chemical farming, and pharmaceutical intervention everywhere. These invading critters give off the most terrible eliminations and odors, which the body will try to push out as best it can. Those with a higher degree of life energy will have the best chances of eliminating them through diarrhea, vomiting, fevers, oozing skin, productive coughs, etc. When these foul eliminations are suppressed, then major trouble begins. Instead of an acute healing crisis, which is, in reality, the body's intelligent pushing out of toxins, chronic and degenerative diseases take hold. At first, the body will try to find ways to at least put toxins in areas considered non-essential to life, such as into the inner ear, tonsils, sinuses, gallbladder, uterus or prostate, but mainly it stores this overload that it can't properly eliminate into fat tissue."

"But these are the areas that are most often treated with drugs or removed entirely by surgery!"

"Oh, for the moment, there will be temporary relief, but it is as if there were a fire smoldering in the basement and the fire alarm went off in the attic. By cutting the wires to the alarm, the annoyance would be silenced, but the deadly fumes would still affect everyone in the house. Thus, the poorly informed victims of such a lifestyle—after years of muddling through life in a fog of fatigue, obesity and depression, all the while suppressing every attempt of their bodies to eliminate the toxins, whether through headaches or skin tags, indigestion or colds—will find that their cells become breached. They become the incurables, born from so-called modern medicine, which takes many to an untimely demise. These are the cancers, the autoimmune disorders, and now the syndromes that perplex even the most schooled healers, currently labeled as chronic fatigue, environmental illness, and fibromyalgia.

"It must be nearly impossible to treat such conditions. I begin to hesitate to want to enter such a realm of misery, as it seems worse now than it was when I was down there last!"

"Not so, dear soul. No matter what the presentation of a disease, the process of the cure is always basically the same. And remember the intelligence within the body itself is the true healer—outer help is only beneficial as it assists the life force to regain its proper flow. Toxins, made from within or coming from without the body, will damage tissue and disrupt functioning of the biological processes. When the toxins are dislodged and the organs of elimination are opened, the liberated tissues will heal by themselves."

Narayan thought deeply and then excitedly commented, "So a true healer is like a gardener. The gardener doesn't make the seed, soil, water or sun, but assists each plant to have the proper balance and timing of each in order to bear the intended fruit, vegetable, grain or flower."

"Well said, my little teacher. And yet another secret is that the true master gardeners are able to telepathically communicate, consciously or by intuition, with the spirits within nature who direct the growth of plant life. Likewise, the best healer is one who, connected to the spirit within all of life, can hold counsel with the intelligence of each organ and gland, with the spirit of each of the lower bodies, and with the flow and balance of the five elements, and can give guidance to the soul that has lost control of the body's functioning. That is why, in the future, the best healers will work on unfolding their spiritual gifts and be open to guidance from above. Then, miraculous healing will become commonplace.

Every animal in the forest knows what herbs to ingest when sick, and when it is time to fast and rest. How much more does man, made in the image of the Divine, have the inner consciousness of the needs of his own vessels of Light? The wisdom of the body can tell the soul directly what is wrong, often through dream images, but for those whose outer mind can't fathom the correct interpretation of these images, the synchronicity of spirit will seek to direct them to the proper healer for their condition, if they are open enough to receiving that type of healing."

CHAPTER 6

Facial Reading & Diagnosis

"But, Goma, is there a quick way get a snapshot of your health in regards to these phases?"

"Indeed there is. And it is as plain as the nose on your face!"

"Nostril diagnosis?"

"No, no—facial reading. You see, Narayan, all creation is holographic in nature."

"I have studied holography. It is quite an exciting area. A laser can form an image in two dimensions and when light is shone through it, it can appear to magically float in three dimensions, but it is entirely made of light."

"That is a perfect description of how we view living bodies on Earth. The light of the Spirit shines through the soul and the four bodies of man appear in their respective spheres, but are entirely made of light vibrating at differing frequencies. The densest light in the physical, atomic particles give the illusion of physicality. In a newborn, the transparency of the form may be glimpsed."

"I also recall that if you are to take any small fragment of the original holographic picture and shine a light through that shard, the living image of the whole picture would be formed, and not merely of the part. It's like how DNA in a single cell becomes a complete person."

"That is a precise description of how the microcosmic diagnostic and treatment methods work, facial diagnosis being one of many—iridology or the study of the iris of the eyes being another. On a cosmic level, we are those fragments, like a drop of water in the ocean of the One God. Each drop has the same essential makeup and quality as the ocean, but in quantity of mass and energy it is incomparably diminished."

"So if the Light of Spirit shines through our purified particle of self, then the whole image of God should be apparent?"

"There you have it—the whole purpose of life! As above, so below."

"But so few seem to have become that fullness of spirit in matter. We know of only a small number of avatars and saints."

"Patience, my dear one, patience. Life is eternal. There is no rush. Each one is on the path to perfection. Each one has the free will to determine their rate of progress. When one strays away from this path, that too can be helpful to them. Then, the nature of reality will assure that circumstances arrange themselves to coax one to make more correct choices."

"So that is the real purpose of illnesses and life's difficulties, to goad us to change direction and return to the path to perfection?"

"In the main, yes, that is true, but those who are on the accelerated path of creativity and spirituality may suffer even more so."

"That seems to be a grand contradiction. Please elaborate on this."

"Most souls on Earth have piled up mountains of karmic debts in their innumerable past lives, as they have gone far afield from the heart of their source. When they finally decide to turn the cycles back in the direction of spirit, it is an uphill climb indeed. The mountain climber cannot have excess baggage when nearing the rarefied heights of the summit. Attachments to material things, emotional connections, and identification with negative mental concepts must be eliminated- often painfully so. On top of this is the karmic return of past sins, both of commission and omission. Added to this is the oppositional attack upon the returning one by entities of darkness that lurk in the lower astral levels of existence surrounding the Earth. Everything on this journey is for the strengthening and purification of the soul, and all is watched carefully from the soul's overshadowing guides on the higher levels. Help is always available to those who ask in faith and sincerity... But enough of our meandering! Back to the map, the magic mask of one's face."

"Yes, of course, what can one learn of his own health and condition by looking in the mirror?"

"I will tell you the basic principles, give you some examples of those in embodiment and have you attempt to divine their conditions. You will have to do some work."

"That sounds fun... Let's begin!"

"First I will show you the basic map of the face. The nose is the center, and thus corresponds to the center of the body, the heart."

"The entire nose?"

"More so the tip. The bridge at the top of the nose is related more to another central organ, the pancreas. The eyes and sight, in general, relate to the liver, although as mentioned, the eye itself portrays a map of entire body. Just as the ears reflect the kidneys, there is a detailed map, really four maps, on the outer ear that show the exact state of health of the entire brain and body. Thus auriculotherapy and acupuncture applied to the *chi* points of the outer ear present another holographic picture."

"Is there no end to these microcosmic maps?"

"Well, there is a map on the nose, the irises and whites of the eyes, the ears, the knee cap, wrist, scalp and foot—and I would venture to say the six feet of DNA, coiled in a fractal pattern in the nucleus of each cell, is the most detailed map of the whole. I would also say that the DNA is a map of one's karma... But you wanted the easiest way to read for the average individual."

"So I did. Forgive my curiosity—it's all just so marvelous and new to me. Let's go back to the face, then: the nose is the heart, the eyes the liver, the ears the kidney. What's next?"

"Under the eyes is a reflection of the kidneys. Between the eyebrows shows the liver. The forehead shows the state of the intestines, the outer portion being the colon and the mid-forehead being the small intestine, just as it is arranged in the body. The skin of the temples has to do with the condition of the spleen. Now, you tell me, if the nose is the heart, what of the cheeks?"

"Let's see, I suppose whatever is to the sides of the heart, which would be the lungs."

"Correct, as well as the breasts in women, which lie on top of them. The mouth reflects the digestive tract in general. What do you think the parts of the lips would denote?"

"You're making me think now. *Hmm*, well the upper lip might correspond to the upper part of the digestive tract, the stomach, and the lower lip, the large bowel?"

"Again correct, and the small intestine is reflected more in the lips inside the mouth."

"So now, tell me. Why did I often get those annoying sores and cracks in the corners of my mouth in my last embodiment?"

"That would correspond to where the small and large intestines are connected, the ileocecal valve and the appendix areas—but a moist, red sore and a dry, whitish crack have opposite causes, as we shall soon see. The last facial area to be mentioned would be the chin, the shape of which has to do with the power of the will of the individual and the skin condition and coloring of this lowest part of the face relate to the lowest of the organs, the sexual glands and structures."

"Wonderful. I understand the basic map. Now, how do I read the meanings of the colors, textures, markings, and discharges of these areas?"

"It's as simple as *yin* and *yang*! Yin would be expansive, loose, wet, red or even purplish in the extreme. *Yang* would be contractive and tight, dry and white. But to understand what is causing these markings, one must understand something of the energetics of the food that is causing them. There is a wide range of foods, from salt, red meat on the *yang* end, to fruit, sugar, alcohol and chemicals on the *yin* side. In the middle lies the grains, vegetables and beans, which all have their own variety within these scales."

"So let's look at the proteins first on this expansion/contraction scale."

"After red meat, poultry would be less contractive and fish even less so, as evidenced by the fact that the more expansive the meat, the less you need a knife to cut it and the less chewing and digestion is involved. Fat, as unfortunately too many know by experience, is expansive; thus, seeds and nuts would be an even more *yin* form of protein, compared to animal foods."

"And what of grains, the staple food of so many cultures?"

"Grains are basically at the balance point energetically and the eating of whole grains won't show up as an imbalance in the face. I would say that the triangular grain of the northern climes, buckwheat, although not technically a cereal grain, would be more *yang* and corn, the tall, sweet, large-kernel grain would be on the *yin* side. Brown rice would hold the balanced middle point in its energetic and nutritional properties."

"What of wheat? It's the most commonly consumed of grains, yet I've heard that it presents a common problem for many. Why is that so?"

"Wheat is almost never eaten in its whole-food state as the wheat berry. It is usually ground into flour, which changes not only the balanced energy of the grain, but also its chemical composition. When the shell of the seed is broken, it is like a capsule of life force that has been broken. The vitality quickly dissipates. The oils within the seed, when in contact with the air, begin to dissi-

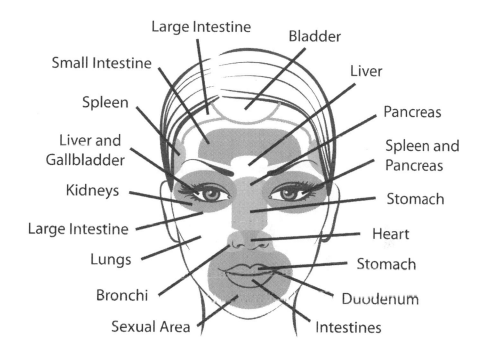

Large Intestine
Bladder
Small Intestine
Liver
Spleen
Pancreas
Liver and Gallbladder
Spleen and Pancreas
Kidneys
Stomach
Large Intestine
Heart
Lungs
Stomach
Bronchi
Duodenum
Sexual Area
Intestines

© WarrenKing.com

pate and deteriorate. Then, perhaps in desire for a longer shelf life, all the beneficial fiber, oils and vitamins are removed and the anemic starch is bleached white and ground to a fine powder. Then, artificially imbalanced laboratory vitamins are added back in, which are never equal in quality to what is found occurring in natural foods. Next, very expansive yeast, sweeteners and often preservatives are added in to make a truly unhealthy concoction. What was once the staff of life has become the acceleration of death.

As far as the problem with wheat in modern society, part of the problem is the quantity consumed. Of the dozen or so grains available, most people eat only two or three on a daily basis, wheat and corn. These are both highly processed, and most likely, grown from genetically modified seeds. These products irritate the mucous membranes of the intestines, which produce more mucous as a protectant. In any condition where there is an excess of mucous or phlegm, eliminating flour products, as well as milk products, is always wise. The pancreas is also inflamed by modern wheat, being part of the source of the diabetes epidemic.

There is also the condition known as *leaky gut*, where the barrier between the intestinal lining and the bloodstream has broken down at microscopic levels, allowing food particles to enter the bloodstream undigested. Whenever the blood detects large protein molecules in the blood, it will see them as foreigners, like bacteria or viruses, and attack. Sometimes, when you eliminate the adverse food reactions, then many allergies to such things as pollen are actually reduced. Even though corn and wheat are common, if one was to eat brown rice and tofu (a non-fermented and therefore less digestible soy product) on a daily basis, then these can become the major allergens. I cannot begin to enumerate the many diseases and complaints these food sensitivities generate, as it depends on the weakness of the particular body."

"Please do give at least a few examples. And please describe what weakens the intestinal barrier in the first place."

"Well, the same parasites, yeast, fungus and harmful bacteria we discussed earlier, are the main culprits in breaking the system down. Tomato and potato, extremely *yin* in character and acidic by nature, often affect the joints of those inclined to weakness there. Many have found a cure to their symptoms of arthritis by simply eliminating these two. Dairy products often harm the respiratory system, and many symptoms of asthma and sinusitis may be resolved by their elimination, as well as by removing the flour products we discussed. In regards to milk products, those studying the explosion of breast cancer would do well to examine the effect of dairy on the breasts, to which they hormonally and energetically correspond.

CHAPTER 7

Your Face Never Lies

Master Goma continued, "The types of food that people typically eat can often be determined on the face itself, Narayan."

"How is that so? Please do tell."

"Let us take tropical fruits as an example. Because of the hot climate they come from, they are very expansive and *yin* in nature and are meant to cool down the systems of the creatures that partake of them. So if someone in the northern climate, who without the convenience of planes and trucks would never naturally partake of these things, consumes bananas and oranges or kiwis and dates on a frequent basis, the *yin* energy would begin to have a noticeable effect—their tissues would become distended and expanded. This would cause an expansion especially of the large intestine and would be seen in a swollen, moist and red lower lip. Gas, bloating, loose stools or even constipation may result if the *yang* force of the peristalsis in the lower intestine is neutralized."

"What if the lower lip is expanded but dry?"

"We must examine what are the most commonly eaten foods. Perhaps they have toast and salted eggs, producing the more dry and contracted energy. Then they may wash it down with orange juice, which is a poor food combination with protein, producing gas, bloating and acid reflux."

"What of heart disease, a most common cause of death for so many? Can we see a forewarning of this by examining the nose?"

"How many could add decades on their life by such attention! If the person is constitutionally or energetically weak, food residue may accumulate there. A devout consumer of butter has a shiny nose; the chronic drinker of fruit juices has a red nose; with soda consumption maybe you will see expanded red capillaries on the nasal tip. With even greater expansion through chronic intake of fermented alcohol, you will have a definite expansion of the entire nose with a purplish hue. With a large intake of salt or animal flesh, you may notice a white nose, indicating a contraction and lack of blood flow, as well as fatty deposits. Red capillaries visible on the sides of the nostrils represent the coronary arteries that are starting to become blocked."

"You mean, if a person was to notice these things and radically alter their diet, their actual nose would change?"

"Yes, this change would be markedly noticeable in a few months. Their blood chemistry would normalize and blood pressure and cholesterol drugs would often be rendered eventually unnecessary. In addition to certain medicinal foods like daikon radish or shiitake mushrooms, often herbs and homeopathic remedies are of great assistance. They would add many good years to their lives that could make the difference in the success of why they came into embodiment in the first place."

"Wow, just nose diagnosis itself could prevent many women from becoming untimely widows!"

"This is true, but remember that, while cardiovascular disease develops seven-to-ten years later in women than in men, today it is still the major cause of death in women over the age of 65 years. So, now you can see, Narayan, why I, who could have specialized in any number of spiritual arts and disciplines, have made nutrition and oriental medicine my specialties. It can mean not only the life and death of the body, but also one's spiritual consciousness can be greatly determined by one's daily diet. As we conclude the study of the nose in facial reading, Narayan, remember that it's just as important to consider the heart on a spiritual level. The heart is the center of love, so any heart problem will point to an imbalance in the flow of that love. Mind you, no one ever says, *I love you from the bottom of my gallbladder!*"

After some hearty laughter, Narayan queried, "Wait, master! Before you go on, I had one more question on the subject of the reading of health through the face."

"What is it?"

"What is the significance of facial spots, either birthmarks or moles, as well as the more transient pimples or acne?"

"Any discharge through the skin is an attempt of the body to eliminate some toxin or excess, when normal channels of elimination are blocked. If the liver or kidneys are backed up, then the skin will take over. Often rashes will occur near areas of greater lymphatic concentration. On the face, the skin will represent the corresponding organs we have discussed. Whiteheads are obviously a discharging of something oily and white... any guesses?"

"How about cheese... ice cream... yogurt... bread and butter... bacon fat?"

"You are a natural at this... and you are quite right. And the redder shades of skin blemishes, more a yin cause. Any candidates you can think of?"

"Oh, many: sugar, honey, beer, tropical fruits, juices, tomato... all come to mind."

"Exactly, but you then must match these by the location. So white pimples on the chin may indicate fatty accumulations in the sexual organs."

"That could give an early indication that there in an imblance there."

"Yes, it may indicate for a woman that a buildup is happening in those organs, and in a man that the prostate may be accumulating toxins. Redness between the eyebrows with white spots and deep creases tells much of a liver under abuse with many different extreme stressors. White spots under the eyes may indicate kidney stones are beginning to form. If swollen, red and baggy under the eyes, it could indicate the kidneys are swollen and burdened, possibly by juices and soda. If a preponderance of white appears under the eyes, there may be too much salt in the diet."

"The possibilities are endless, as the variety of faces to be seen on Earth can testify."

"Yes, and the faces of babies as still not poisoned by the foods of the day, shine beautifully. Birthmarks often represent the diet of the mother during pregnancy, as does the entire physiognomy of the face itself. If an excess of animal protein is consumed, then the child's liver may not be able to handle it and a *yang* discharge, perhaps a dark, hardened mole may have appeared on the brow, or on the nose if the heart was more vulnerable. Red spots may likewise appear on the face or anywhere along the acupuncture meridians if more sugary *yin* foods were partaken of in excess. But these are just the physical levels of interpretation. There are also symbols of karma and ancient traumas remaining in the finer bodies that can show themselves on the body as birthmarks or defects."

"This is all so interesting! What of the general shape of the face and the arrangement of its parts that make each person look so unique?"

"It is good to study the embryonic development of the child in the womb, especially as you will soon be undergoing such an experience yourself in the near future. Each feature develops at different times during gestation. The eyes, for example, start out at the sides of the head, like a fish, and gradually converge toward the front of the face. If under a more *yin* or expansive influence, the eyes will be larger and farther apart. If under a more contractive *yang* energy, the eyes will be smaller and closer together."

"These general features of the facial layout and the diet of the mother during pregnancy tell much about the person and influence their destiny to some extent."

"Oh, if only mothers would prepare their temples better for the coming of the little ones and eat in a balanced way during pregnancy, a new race of beautiful and healthy people would soon result! The basic constitution as seen on the face and determined not only by the genes, which are karmic tendencies in coded form, but by the diet itself, can have an immense bearing on the mission of each soul and the health of the body that will be its vehicle."

CHAPTER 8

Constitution vs. Condition

"**D**ear Goma, what exactly do you mean by *constitution*? I really want to understand this concept, it sounds highly important."

"Important, yes, as it is the key to health. The constitution is the basic makeup and strength of the body—its fiber, if you will. Some people are made of hard wood, like an oak tree, others of soft pine. A hardwood floor can take a beating, needs less care, and won't dent or scratch easily. A floor of a softer wood will tend to split, mold, pit and generally deteriorate at a faster rate. So it is with the body. A person of strong constitution can weather life's storms with less stress. They will often even thrive under conflict and get bored in times of ease. They feel a reserve of energy in the body and expect it to serve without tiring and falling ill. If they ever do catch a cold, which is rare, after a few sneezes and a long sleep, it would pass. They can eat and drink almost anything and never feel worse for it afterwards."

"Oh, I'll take one of those bodies, please!"

"If only your menu were not quite so, complex, shall we say?"

"So, if someone has a strong constitution, they can do anything they want against the natural laws of health and get away with it?"

"For a time, yes, but not forever. Besides a constitution, which is your hereditary energy, there is your *condition*, which is your current status at any given point in time. This waxes and wanes, and unfortunately for most, declines with age."

"Can you explain in greater detail this concept of condition?"

"A list of symptoms that present themselves at present is a good indicator of one's condition. In the facial diagnosis we discussed, indicators of one's inherited constitution include the size of the ears, the nose, the spacing between the eyes, and a chin that is either projecting or receding. These are indicators of constitution. The passing scenes of spots, discolorations and discharges are pictures of one's condition, and can be readily altered. The major landmarks on one's face cannot be altered without surgery."

"So does constitution have to do with one's family genetics and history, as family members tend to look like one another, as well as getting similar health problems?"

"Well, a family may have certain weakness, for instance, the pancreas may be weak, or the joints. Family members may tend toward hypoglycemia, diabetes, or arthritis. But if during pregnancy a mother eats foods that do not bring stress to these organs, in this case avoiding refined sugars and minimizing nightshade vegetables, such as tomatoes and potatoes, then there will be less stress on these organs as they form in the womb...

"And don't forget that while members of a family share the same genes, they also often share the same basic diet and emotional patterns—plus there is the fact that genes mutate and alter based on the frequencies of the thoughts and emotions of the indwelling soul, making it possible to gradually transmute the genetic makeup, or make it so undesirable traits are never activated. DNA itself is acidic, and as in a battery, the surrounding fluids must be alkaline. If these fluids become acidified due to diet or toxic buildup, then the genes can either alter from their

intended pattern, resulting in cancer, or the immune system can begin to attack these intercellular toxins- resulting in autoimmune diseases."

"So even these diseases may be cured? Many thousands of bikeathons and walkathons have hardly made a dent in these conditions."

"You never tire of questions, Narayan! Well, then I shall never tire of giving answers, although we are wandering from the topics of condition, but very well. The process of healing is always the same. Firstly, clear the organs of elimination to drain toxins to the outside. Secondly, dislodge toxins from their storage sites on the inside of the body in the organs, tissues and cells, and push them out their proper exits. Thirdly, get good nutrition to the cells. This involves not only diet, but also proper hydration, digestion, circulation and respiration. Fourthly, work on the mental, emotional and spiritual patterns that allowed the organs to stagnate and the toxins to deposit in the first place."

"So why has modern science had so little result with so much time and money spent?"

"I don't want to say all of modern medicine is negative, much research has been sponsored by advanced beings and many medicines are indeed lifesavers, but as far as treating the root causes, they are barking up the wrong tree, as they say. The whole basis of healing these conditions is the elimination of toxins. This is readily accomplished with lifestyle changes and the use of plants in herbology and homeopathy. But due to the greed of the companies and institutions that profit from sickness, these keys are ignored, not because they cannot be proven, but because you cannot patent a leaf and make billions from selling it. A good portion of these chemical drugs have been derived from plants, but they are so hyper-purified as to throw off the entire balance put there by nature, and by their extreme action they produce numerous side effects, many worse than the original complaint itself.

This chemical masking of symptoms does not produce a cure, and unfortunately, it was not intended to. What you see instead is the suppression of symptoms of the body's attempt to cleanse itself of these highly acidic substances in order to regain balance. Detoxifying the organs and cells are key to deeper healing, as well as addressing the underlying causes of mental and emotional patterns, and then the underlying karma itself."

"It's hard for me to grasp all of this. Can you please give me an example as might be seen in a real case?"

"Certainly, just visit any chronically ill person in modern society and you will likely see the same unfortunate story. It might look something like this: a child is born into a typical family that is uncomfortable in dealing with its emotions. As he starts the expression of his sense of sadness, grief and anger in the normal frustrations of infancy, such as sitting in a wet diaper, or getting a stomachache from the indigestible formula made of an allergenic base of milk or soy, with loads of sugary corn syrup and low-quality vegetable fats, he may seem to the parent that he is crying too much. So he hears, first gently and later with greater emphasis, 'Don't cry, baby. *Shhhhh...* Stop crying already!' When out of shock he suddenly is silenced, he then hears the tender voice with the gentle caress, 'Good boy. I love you. You are so good.' Thus after many repetitions in various scenarios, the child starts to learn that when he suppresses his natural tendency to express his feelings in an overt way, or pays undue attention to the clues his body is giving him that something is not right or that he is bad. When he is quiet and pleasing to the adults around him, he is good."

"Well, Goma, this really interests me. I feel that my own mission lies more with the understanding of the soul and its emotions than with the body. So what does happen to the emotions and feelings when they are suppressed and not let out?"

"Some will learn to put that pressure into their mental bodies and talk about their feelings, but will not actually feel or express them emotionally anymore. Thus sometimes they can find help in changing their situation. However, by denying the emotions—the energy-in-motion—between their thoughts and their body, they live more in the mind and are focalized in the head and not the body, leaving the chakras and their corresponding glands and organs with less vital energy with which to function."

"And what of those who do not even deal with these feelings in a mental way?"

"Instead of allowing a release valve of expression by way

of speech, the energy is stuffed in the body, and pressure begins to build. Often the energy will go to the corresponding organ and tissues related to the five phases of transformation we have studied."

"*Ahhh*, I see. Let me try to remember... repressed anger would effect a degeneration of the liver, gallbladder and their corresponding areas of the eyes, as well as the tendons and ligaments or meridian areas along the inner and outer legs and chest. Worry and over-thinking would weaken the spleen, pancreas, and stomach giving both digestive and blood sugar imbalances, as well as muscle weakness or weight disorders. Fear and anxiety would weaken the kidneys and bladder, and might even lead to fatigue, dark circles under the eyes, allergies, incontinence or back pain. Lack of joy might weaken the heart, which might cause speech problems like stuttering, or small-intestine issues, rendering assimilation of food inefficient. Suppressed grief would target the lungs or large intestine, causing a wide variety of problems, from frequent colds, cough or asthma to constipation, diarrhea, gas and bloating."

"My, my, Narayan, you do learn fast! I am pleased. You may find on Earth that it takes hours, days or weeks or even longer to learn what may take an instant here. So, in this case, let us say that this child had a somewhat strong constitution. The tension in the body, after weakening the naturally deep breathing of the baby and slowing down the enzymes of digestion, started to allow some acidity and toxicity to build in the system. Immediately this would signal the body intelligence to find the quickest avenue of exit. Thus, the toxic irritations would stimulate the body to produce mucus as a protectant, and this would seek an exit, either from the lungs through coughing or through the sinuses, which often are outlets for intestinal toxicity. If allowed to drain outward in this way, there might be no further problem after a few days, and if the same diet and emotional suppression was continued, then periodically the body might cleanse itself periodically."

"I assume that's why young children have frequent colds, as they are striving to cleanse themselves, but this is not so successfully accomplished by the person who ends up chronically ill and on numerous medications.

"Well, that is partially true, but the immune system is hopefully practicing and learning what is self and what is not self. This is nature's inoculation, and the white blood cells will remember what to do for next time. But when illness is too frequent, when ear infections linger, or tonsils are repeatedly inflamed, then it is often a toxicity issue. If the toxicity and acidity continue long enough, they will attract the ever-present bacteria, viruses, parasites and fungi that seek such an environment. Now, the parents take notice because the mucous is not clear, but yellow or green, and the breathing passages are chronically impeded.

"The immune system will heat up the body to burn out the invaders, and the mucous membranes will start discharging as white blood cells are rapidly streaming through them to the battle sites. And guess what? After a few days or a week, the body will be victorious, and balance will be regained. Again, if the emotions are still suppressed, and the diet incompatible with nature, this battle might have to be waged a few times each year."

"So, is this a disease? How does it become a chronic problem?"

"You may call it *dis-ease* if you want, for the body is not feeling at ease, but that doesn't make it a problem. This is the body seeking homeostasis—to find balance again. If allowed to cleanse periodically, the toxins should not accumulate enough to start damaging tissues and certainly not to damage the internal structures of the cells themselves. This is just an acute, short-lived readjustment. It only becomes chronic when not allowed to proceed to completion, when the toxins are not allowed to be eliminated completely or when the battle against the invaders is prematurely stopped, either by suppressing the immune system or by fighting the bugs with an external agent, signaling to the body that it can retire its weapons of defense."

"Are you saying, then, that the normal reaction of parents to give a nose spray, a cough medicine, an antihistamine or a pill to lower a fever can actually lead the body of that child on the pathway to chronic disease and degeneration?"

"Of course, this is never the conscious intention. All parents feel they must do something to relieve the suffering of the little ones under their care—and the mind-set of applying a medicine is well implanted in this society. For those children with strong systems, often rest and water is all that is needed, the body will take the lead. If the body is not hungry, it is asking for fasting. Don't force it to eat; it is usually that simple. For those who are a bit weaker or for parents who absolutely must do something, Mother Nature has provided a bountiful herbal pharmacy for all the needs of the body. There are many remedies that can assist the body in its process of cleaning house. But remember, their use must not be to just get rid of the symptom, but to assist the body's ability to self-cleanse.

Thus, if the body is weakened and can only get to a fever of 100° Fahrenheit, a careful homeopathic dose of the plant aconitum might stimulate the fever to surge to 103° and then break, but a dose of aspirin or antibiotics might unnaturally stop the process of cooking out the bugs, leaving the infections inactive, hiding in pockets and gathering strength. It might leave the immune system confused, and in a weaker state than before. In a very small percentage of cases where the system is too run down, or the infection is too strong and the natural remedies are insufficient, then the administration of drugs is indicated."

CHAPTER 9

The Microbiome & Healing's Future

"Oh, yes, Master Goma, I've heard that there is worry on Earth of *superbugs* forming from the overuse of antibiotics that are universally dispensed."

"True, but this is not yet the problem for the average individual. The real damage comes from the antibiotics that do not discriminate in terms of which types of bacteria they destroy. As you may know, bodies are made of all sorts of organisms that cooperate to help themselves survive, as well as their host, the body as a whole.

Some organisms are part of the body itself, like white blood cells or sperm cells, which seem like unicellular, free, living creatures, but are produced by the body and dedicated to its service, even at their own expense. Some are acquired externally, such as the helpful *acidophilus* and *bifidus* probiotic bacteria that thrive in healthy mucous membranes, especially the digestive tract and the colon in particular. These beneficent microorganisms assist in digestion and produce certain vitamins essential for health. They also act in holding a vital niche in the body's ecology. If they are destroyed for any reason, then there is a vacuum, and as you know, nature abhors a vacuum. So other, more malicious creatures—the fungi, yeast, harmful bacteria, viruses and parasites—find an easier foothold."

"Are there other ways that people discourage the friendly flora and invite the unwelcome fauna?"

To answer your question, antibiotics are the most extreme threat to a healthy gut, and these are even found in industrially farmed animals that have been given these substances to keep them alive long enough to make it to market. Taking birth control pills, hormonal replacements, steroids, cortisone, and drinking tap water with chemicals such as chlorine all serve to throw off the internal balance of these organisms."

"Short of a laboratory examination, how would one know that they have been so invaded and compromised?"

"Strong cravings for sugar and sweets, for fermented and aged foods like alcohol, vinegar, soy sauce, yeasty breads, mushrooms, chocolate, and acidic foods like tomato sauce and orange juice are sure signs that a yeast invasion and candida overgrowth is well underway. Experiencing gas, bloating and varied digestive problems such as constipation or diarrhea will confirm their nasty presence."

"Are there foods that can encourage the beneficial flora?"

"Indeed there are! All societies have enjoyed foods teeming with good bacteria. In Korea, they have *kimchi*, in Germany sauerkraut, many places have fermented milk products like *kefir*. In Japan they use *miso*, and many people today are enjoying the ancient Chinese *kombucha*, a fermented tea drink."

"I'll have to make sure I get some of these fermented foods in my diet. So, getting back to our case, what would be a likely solution for a body after the lungs or sinuses have been suppressed from eliminating their toxic load?"

"The skin has a direct connection to the lungs with their internal mucous membranes, which are actually as large as a tennis court in surface area. The skin is somewhat thicker and dryer, but it can be used in a pinch as a secondary route of discharge."

"So, you are saying that someone who has been on antihistamines, cough suppressants, or allergy medicine might start developing skin diseases like rashes, eczema, psoriasis, acne, or even boils?"

"I would not call them diseases—just another avenue of discharge. But since there is a time lag between when the toxins were pushed deeper and when they were able to be erupted through the skin, rarely are the two events connected in sequence by those experiencing them."

"I suppose this new problem would have to be dealt with by using a new medicine. Perhaps a cream would clear up these annoying, unattractive and often itchy skin irritations."

"That is true. There are a few natural substances such as the cream of the calendula flower, or Mary's Gold, that can assist the body in ridding the acidic toxins through the skin, or an absorbent, such as clay. But even these should not be needed for more than a few days. If the problem persists, the cause that is generating the release of these toxins has not been addressed. Many will blindly try a stronger medicine, steroids being the strongest, that will drive the poisons even further inward. You will notice that it is where lymph tissue is most concentrated that skin problems often erupt. These are areas where the body can most easily find a vent to the surface."

"So, what happens if the skin and lungs are both foiled in their attempts to discharge the toxic residue?"

"Another exit will have to be found. It might be from the lower end, through gas or loose bowels, or through an upper channel, vomiting or sinus discharge, through the eyes, or ear oozing. Natural healers can read the body and assist in this discharge process by stimulating and clearing the main elimination organs, such as the kidney, liver, and intestines, to function more efficiently with many tools such as acupuncture, homeopathy, massage, baths, etc. They will encourage the patient to clean house—fasting may be used and other methods to purify the blood and all bodily systems, but the vast majority of modern people will blindly end up on the suppressive route using stronger and stronger medications."

"But, won't the body's intelligence continue to find creative ways to eliminate whatever it needs to?"

"Oh yes, the body is very creative. But, as fast as it devises new avenues of cleansing, people have found more ways to misunderstand the entire process. Thus, the average person, after having body parts removed, is on at least a half-dozen prescriptions by the time they're 60 years old. You see, the body will first squirrel away the toxins into areas that it considers least important for survival. The nervous system must be protected, as well as the heart, so it will fill up the gallbladder with sludge, store it in fat tissue under the skin, in the uterus or prostate, in breast tissue, or in sinus cavities. The stench of the accumulated rubbish automatically signals to the various microorganisms that an attractive home has been set up for them, just as flies seem to locate a dung heap from miles away.

"It is at this stage that the person will clearly know that something is not right. The sensitive and intuitive healer can easily find these areas that have been burdened since childhood, decades before they would ever be found on a laboratory test or radiological scan, and reverse the process in just a few weeks or months. In more severe cases, in may take a few years of right living, feeling and thinking to recreate health out of many decades of abuse, with a few natural remedies applied to speed the process."

"Are you actually saying that the hospitals, surgeons and pharmacies would be twiddling their thumbs—or perhaps go out of business—if this more natural form of living and healing were practiced from childhood?"

"Oh, we shall see an entire transformation of the healthcare system even in your next lifetime and we shall make sure that all are busily engaged in the mighty work of restoring health to the bodies of God's children. Up here, we prepare the movements of things centuries and even millennia before they manifest on Earth. It is like a cosmic chess game.

We have introduced the scientific method so that only what truly works and is beneficial to the people is maintained. There are those who have taken the heart and spirit out of science and have denied the first rule of maintaining an open mind in all investigations. Those who have used profit as their only motive and have brought the mounting health crisis upon the nations will not prevail.

We have sent our specially trained souls, many who are ready to take their places and those who are just finishing their medical training. They have a compassionate heart, an open mind, and are willing to look objectively at the results of natural healing, right eating, and right thinking. Even if they don't quite understand the detailed mechanisms of action, they will heartily apply all techniques that benefit their patients and, as written in their Hippocratic oath, to first, do no harm. They will broaden their awareness beyond the ultra-thin slice of physical vibrations and shall, in time, see how true healing occurs in various dimensions of reality.

We are sponsoring the next advancements, which now appear under the name of *functional medicine*. This is laboratory testing based on the scientific understanding of how cells and organs function. It uses mostly natural and nutritional products to treat the physical causes."

"We are inspiring researchers to study the role of the microbiome in health, where the cells of all the organisms that make up the body are taken into consideration. Can you believe that for every single cell in the human body, there are ten times more other organisms assisting its functioning? In addition, many of our students are now scientifically proving how meditation, mindfulness and prayer are key players in improving one's health."

"Oh, I am so excited to be able to see real health finally manifesting on our dear planet Earth. Illness and disease have seemed to dominate the scene for all of history."

"At least during the brief time that is recorded in the history books since Egypt and Sumeria were at their heights. But, if you were to look into the true and ancient history of Earth before recorded history, to Altantis, Lemuria and beyond, to the time when the first humans were on this planet, you would see there were great expanses of time where Golden Ages reigned and all were aware of the reality of their inner Great God Self. In this positive vibration and consciousness, the body itself had much less density. It was more luminous, and there was no place for the darkness of degeneration to take hold."

"Then the Biblical reference to Methuselah and others living many hundreds of years was not mere allegory?"

"No, this was a literal reality. Enlightened man did not die so much as he consciously left his form when his Spirit beckoned him to new adventures and greater frequencies of existence for his next step in evolution... Oh, I see you have a visitor patiently waiting for you."

CHAPTER 10

Meeting Sephira

I t was dear Baltar, his own teacher, admiring the rapidly expanding awareness in the etheric brain of his beloved pupil. Beside him stood a young woman, tall and stately, her jade-hued robe hanging elegantly around her well-proportioned form. To Narayan, she seemed to be the most intriguing woman he had ever seen. He tried to control his aura so as not to emit too much excitement at seeing such perfection and grace, but was woefully unsuccessful.

Baltar pretended not to notice Narayan's reaction. Goma remarked, "I am well-pleased with your student, Baltar. He learns quickly. Please call on me if ever he should need further illumination on health or diet while in embodiment."

Then he raised his hands as Narayan instinctively knelt humbly before him and intoned a sacred mantra of resonant vowels, used only by high initiates in the etheric retreats for the sponsoring of disciples in the empowerment of healing. Narayan became aware of a cascading river of light descending upon him, tingling every particle of his being. He saw only white light, tinged with the emerald ray of his holy order.

"From now on, you are not only a soul therapist but also healer of the physical form. May compassion ever be your guide in your journey of life!"

To Narayan's surprise, Goma merely disappeared into a single point—a tiny, shining star of radiating light, sparking in all directions and then, *blink...* he was gone.

"Wow, he is quite a teacher!" he exclaimed. Then, in an aside, he whispered to Baltar behind his hand, knowing full well that there were no secrets in Heaven, "But I thought I was in the business of healing the soul."

Baltar replied, "The same laws govern all phenomena, and I suppose when the master looked down through your lifestream and saw your potential to do good, he decided it was worth planting some seeds, so you could adapt some of your methods for the healing of the body as well. In incarnation, it is hard to separate a person's soul from their brain and their body. Besides, your parents know next to nothing about health or nutrition and your entire life's plan may depend upon your finding your own path to healing."

"Well, I can recall a few lifetimes of poor health and I remember how hard it was to have a clear mind or positive emotions when I was feeling physically awful. Isn't there some trick to earning myself a good constitution?"

"It goes back to the ancient motto: *To gain one's life, one must first lose it—or give it away.*"

"That is very poetic, but what does it really mean?"

To Narayan's delight, it was the intriguing woman who took up the conversation. In a melodic voice that thrilled him to his very soul, she said, "It is my experience that those who are the most generous and those who share with others, even the little that they have, those who go the extra mile to serve others, those are the ones that end up being graced with the best constitutions in their future incarnations."

"I would suppose that you have had a few nice bodies yourself... I mean, you know, good constitutions..."

Baltar quickly saved his student from his embarrassing stumble of words, "My son, I neglected to introduce you to one of my students, this is Sephira. Sephira, this is Narayan."

She gently bowed with hands before her, as in prayer, strands of her long golden hair framing her sparkling yet gentle green eyes. "It's a pleasure to be reacquainted with a fellow student on the path," she said sweetly.

Narayan, returned the gesture, trying to hide his disappointment at not holding her hand, yet relieved that if he did, he might tremble or grasp it too tightly. As she smoothed her hair back behind her ear, he realized that he had said nothing as he was absorbed in his own thoughts. She merely said with a smile, "Likewise, I'm sure." He could have sworn he felt a kiss upon his cheek and an embrace, heart to heart. But he blinked twice, and it was clear that she had never moved. But that voice! Where had he heard it before? It was so familiar, as if it had always been a part of him.

Baltar put his hand on Narayan's shoulder and began to explain, "You do not remember all your lives just now, but Sephira has played a significant role in many of them, having been your sister, your wife, your aunt, your mother, and often a lover. However, this time she is to be your friend. You will grow up in the same neighborhood and become lifelong friends. It is like a buddy system—if either of you gets too off track with your life-plan, the other will provide a voice of reason, support and sanity in an often-insane world. But remember, no *hanky panky*. If you try to get into romance, then it may spoil this special bond you have and make it difficult to remain long-term friends, not only with each other, but with your spouses!"

Baltar paused to let this sink in, then continued, "Narayan, the timing of Sephira's entrance and Goma's departure is no coincidence, for you see, Sephira has been working on a course of study that dovetails perfectly with your own.

Sephira herself broke in to continue the thought, "I was wondering if I might be able to share my insights with you, so you will know of my mission and I of yours, in order that we may never forget our main purpose in the world."

Narayan replied, "Well spoken, sister. I would like to hear of your wisdom and would consider it an honor to be your lifelong friend."

Baltar patted them both on the shoulders, "Well done, my children. You will have plenty of time later to continue your conversation, but now you are both summoned to a special meeting."

Narayan had a few moments to pose a question to Baltar that had been in his mind for some time: "Baltar, what is Sephira to me? Are we soul mates?"

Baltar answered, "On Earth, when two individuals are in a committed, long-term relationship, there are usually three main scenarios. Either they are soul mates, meaning they have a high affinity with each other's souls and a mission to accomplish together, or there's a karmic relationship, or they are twin flames. The close bond with a soul mate usually takes several embodiments to attain. They often work together between lives and are in the same soul group, which is like a big, extended family whose members are frequently drawn to embody along with each other.

"Having a soul mate on Earth is a wonderful boon, as you can serve together and work on common projects, whether it be raising a family, running a business enterprise, or being pillars of a community. So, Narayan, while you and Sephira will always be soul mates, that's not quite the setup for your next earthly life.

"What you will have is a karmic marriage, which is very common nowadays. If there is unfinished business between two souls, they may take a vow at inner levels to work it out. This enables them to stay together when the difficult issues surface and hopefully, they will ride it out until that karma has been balanced. Since world karma is being sped up, many people will have more than one karmic relationship to deal with. Often, when the karma has been balanced, they will feel it and know that it's time to part ways. Of course, this is best done with forgiveness and grace, not with animosity or revenge, so as not to create more karmic ties."

"But do I have an eternal mate—that one-and-only soul who is just for me?"

"Yes, indeed! That would be what we call your twin flame or twin ray. When souls first begin their journey, the original God Flame divides itself into two equal and complementary polarities, while still maintaining that eternal connection. Early on in evolution, twin flames were always paired together, but over the eons, many were separated and made karma and connections with others. They became lost to each other, at least on the outer. That is the feeling many souls have of always searching for their one and only, but alas, they are not always available to incarnate at the same time, of the same age, and in the same place."

"And can I dare ask what has happened to my twin flame?"

"For some of us, it's a somewhat sad situation where the twin flame is at a lower level and we have to wait long periods until they evolve back to our level. But in your case, Narayan, it's a happier story. Your twin flame is already a liberated, ascended being. She earned her freedom after her time on Atlantis. She is now in a period of rest and recharge in Nirvana, in the Great Silence, which is similar to a restorative, dreamless sleep. She is in complete bliss and oneness with the Universe and her God Presence. She will step forth into individuality again when you are about to start your mission. She will overshadow and protect your work. You will then be able to be with her while you sleep, although you may only awake with a feeling of that completeness.

"After this life, if all goes well, you will also earn your ascension. Then you will be reunited forevermore, both with each other and with your God Flame, which will greatly accelerate your potential and power as God-Beings to continue your service in the ascended state."

Narayan felt quite satisfied with these explanations and pondered these things in his heart. He continued on in silence in anticipation of the upcoming meeting.

CHAPTER 11

Blessing of Souls on the 7 Rays

All laughed heartily as they entered the meeting hall. There were perhaps eighty altogether in the room—teachers and students milling about, chatting in small groups. Their group was among the last to arrive and when all were present, a tone rang out throughout the room, signaling all to take their seats. Two great masters, well known but seldom seen at these levels, stood at the head of the table, which was oval in shape and made of what seemed like a violet jade with veins of green snaking throughout it. The walls were also of a highly polished, marble-like material with opposite shading, a self-luminous translucent green with violet veins running throughout. Embossed in the walls were patterns of gold flecked with diamonds. They formed shapes that at once seemed to be conveying the constellations of the zodiac, but also the geometric shapes that underlie the sub-molecular world, as if to convey the concept that the macrocosmic and microcosmic worlds are one, and there is but one all-intelligent, powerful and loving Life.

Again, Narayan's and indeed everyone's attention fell upon these two magnificent beings that had convened this gathering. Even the statues of the Greek gods of old couldn't compare with the majesty and grandeur that this pair emitted. They were clothed in what seemed to be scintillating jewels whose sparkle and glow merged in what appeared to be living flames that leaped and danced in their aura of joyous self-mastery.

Baltar, sensing his pupil's awe and wonder, telepathically whispered to his mind, "These are the two cosmic beings—twin flames, now united as one with their great God Flame—who built this retreat ages ago and whose service has moved on to the creation of new solar systems within our galaxy. But one day, we shall all be as such and they too will move on in the eternal cycles of being. Remember, Narayan—what one has done, all can do."

Narayan whispered to Baltar, "I can sense they have a deep humility, as if they were the servants of all."

They raised their staffs, which appeared to be of a silvery-gold metal unknown to Earth, with a large faceted emerald on top of his and a clear crystal sphere on hers. On top of these radiating stones stood depictions of two thoughtforms.

Atop the master's staff stood a caduceus, like the one that Moses raised in the wilderness for healing, and which is still the emblem of healers today, representing the raising of the energies along the spine, bringing both enlightenment and healing. The rod in the center was of yellow gold and the twin serpents that wound about it were of intense pink and electric blue. These three colors represented the three-fold flame of the heart—the love, wisdom and power that must be balanced before the cosmic energies and vibrations of the kundalini can be raised up.

Above the crystal of the lady master's somewhat more slender staff rested the form of a dove, which, although made of a whitish pink crystalline material, seemed to have a life of its own and gave the impression of being warm and soft. A blissful light emanated from these two beings with their raised staffs, as an intense peace and joy descended upon all.

As they welcomed all the guests, the master spoke, "Our dear friends, we have convened this feast in honor of you brave and noble souls, many who will shortly take the courageous descent to Earth. You have seen the inhabitants' plight of illness and ignorance, and through your chosen paths as healers, scientists and bearers of truth, you will seek to bring relief from suffering. For this, you have earned our blessing and protection."

Narayan stood in awe and in rapt attention. He felt his consciousness so raised that he could actually see through the walls and ceiling to see what seemed like other interpenetrating dimensions of the Heaven worlds. He explained, "We now open your vision to the other 'Mansions of our Father,' where many souls, whose emphasis is on one of the other six rays, are preparing for the grand entrance for the plan of Earth's salvation. For although we two, among the fourteen guardians of Earth and her evolutions, have long prepared for and predicted the coming of a great Golden Age of love and peace, illumination and grandeur, we, although strong in the power of our Father/Mother God, can do little to influence the free will of mankind. For free will is mankind's birthright as divine sparks of God. Thus you, one with that Lord, will also embody the freedom to choose upon Earth, and through the God in you, the Great I AM, will turn the tide of wrong choices and desires, and assist the many to build that which we have envisioned for ages.

"Right now, there are similar gatherings in all the retreats of our Brotherhood. For you, the future scientists and doctors, inventors and healers will not be alone to assist in the upward progress of the Earth. Unlike here in the higher octaves where like attracts like and you all serve and learn together, upon Earth you will be dispersed and work as a widespread mandala of souls with those of the other paths and rays of service."

"It is important that you learn to respect and work together with those who have other specializations on Earth. All are being reminded that, although life is meant to be pleasurable, the fixation on seeking pleasure and ease can no longer be the goal of those whom we allow to incarnate. We need to rely on those who want to work hard in righting the ship of Earth."

Then the beautiful lady master put her hand on his shoulder, as he stepped back and allowed her to continue as the energy in the room softened. As she stood there, a little fairy about three inches tall, flitted about her and landed on the top of the dove on her staff and whispered in her ear for a moment as she nodded in assent. Hushed laughter was heard around the room.

She continued, "I am reminded to tell you that it is not for humanity alone that you are sent to Earth. Behind the scenes, there are trillions of elementals, the nature spirits that keep the foundation of your evolution and all of nature functioning smoothly. They want me to remind you that besides your specific service to life, all are responsible for stopping pollution, not only in the physical as in chemicals, plastics and heavy metals, but also the emotional pollution as in anger, fear and hatred, which also burdens the sensitive bodies of these tender spirits." With that, the fairy folded her arms across her chest, gave one exaggerated nod, and flew off. This elicited a chorus of giggles throughout the room.

"Now, as I was saying, there are many meetings happening simultaneously..." Just then an angel flew down and hovered at her side, whispering in her other ear for some moments. "So now, the angels want equal time." At this, all laughed.

"This one wants me to convey to you that the angels are being frustrated in their attempts to help mankind. They have a sacred trust in ministering to those on Earth. The cosmic law states that they can only help when invited by a person's free-will request. Thus, be reminded that you must pray daily to God to send his angels to minister to those who need assistance and pray especially for the children and babies in the womb, among whom you shall soon be counted.

"The angels also want to remind you to pray for God's Will to act upon those who have stolen the light of God and use it to control, manipulate and enslave the minds, bodies and souls of those on Earth." Looking satisfied, the angel ascended, leaving behind a shimmering light that descended upon all in the room.

"As I was saying..." she paused and looked around. When sure of no other winged messengers, she continued, "There are meetings such as ours happening simultaneously in other retreats. Many others who are soon incarnating are being addressed by their most advanced teachers as well.

"There are those who will gain the mastery of power in the Will of God. These will be servant leaders, governmental officials,

91

lawmakers and police officers, upholding and precipitating the laws of our Father on Earth as it is in Heaven. From our perspective, it is the most humble and selfless among us who may earn the right and the authority to lead, govern and direct others.

"Then there are those who will master the ray of illumination and wisdom. These wise ones are ready to bring to Earth a renaissance of the ancient wisdom, fused with the advancements in the mind and technology that have been released on Earth in recent decades. These are the teachers and educators, philosophers and thinkers of the ages. They will transform education, beginning in the womb, and show how the education of the whole person—heart, head and hand—is what teaching is all about and not merely the filling of the brain with information.

"Also incarnating are those full of love who are to outpicture the beauty of their souls to the world of form. Without beauty, life is like a desert and the soul becomes hard and shriveled. Without love, there is no reason for existence, for all was created in love, for love, and by love. They are emboldened and prepared to transform every environment they touch, whether grand or humble, in order to reflect the beauty within. Whatever the form, in art, dance, the spoken or written word, entertainment or media, may they all bring souls upward into the Light.

"Then there are those who are the warriors of the spirit who are willing to risk life and limb for the defending of the helpless and downtrodden. There are also those who will aid in the construction of buildings, towns, cities, roads and bridges, reflective of the realms of spirit.

"And of course, there are also going forth many precious souls who live merely to serve, demonstrating by humble example that those who *have* the most *give* the most. They support all, encourage all, love all, and yet claim nothing for themselves. They pray, sacrifice and serve until all with whom they are karmically tied achieve their own goals and destinies. These ministering servants are equally content in Heaven or Earth, as long as they know they are assisting their brothers and sisters on the pathway of life.

You may recognize them in the understanding ear of the hairstylist or the smiling checkout clerk at the supermarket.

"Most heart-wrenching of all is the example of one of our most advanced initiates who decided to take birth as an unknown Down syndrome child, who will hold the balance for his entire country and thereby prevent both war and cataclysm. But alas, he has been aborted twice so far, due to preemptive genetic testing. Just because a child has health challenges, doesn't mean that the soul has not chosen this situation."

There was not a dry eye in the room and all vowed within themselves never to judge anyone, especially the infirm or handicapped, by their outer appearance.

"Then there are those who will bring in the spiritual teaching that is the hallmark of the Aquarian Age. There will be priests and rabbis, monks and nuns, disciples and teachers. They will break down the barriers between the world's religions and teach all to contact the God Within who dwells in each beating heart. Prejudice and superstition will be swept aside by the great incoming Cosmic Light. All will respect the spiritual path of their fellow beings. More and more, people will espouse core spiritual principles that will be freely chosen rather than determined by race or birth. They will take what truth they perceive from different spiritual paths, according to their inner promptings and nature."

Then the masters sounded forth their eloquent blessing:

You of the heart of God's emerald-green flame, go forth unto the children of Terra. Open their eyes that those in darkness may see the inner light of the soul. Bring forth the wonderful advancements in healing of body, mind, feelings and soul, which you have so diligently pursued and discovered during your interval in these realms of wisdom.

Show them the path back to nature and to rediscover how the Divine Mother has placed all medicines and remedies in the minerals and plants that are made abundantly available to all. Unfold to them the glorious future of technology, which will advance even beyond the glory days of Atlantis, where lasers and the application of frequencies will readjust the cellular structure to align with the inner blueprint of the perfect etheric body.

Bring forth your wondrous inventions to help lift all from the drudgery of life, that their time might be used for the pursuing of individual and collective genius, enlightenment and beauty on Earth, as it is done here in Heaven. Speak truth in every domain and bring the media of communication that we have released to Earth back to its intended purpose, for the upliftment and betterment of all, lifting all aspects of modern entertainment up from the mire of the lower astral plane into the light.

Along with those gaining mastery on all of the seven rays, may you work together to build a culture such as the Earth has never seen. May the Love, Wisdom and Divine Will of God be upon you in the full purity of spiritual service, that you might proclaim the truth to all—and that the truth may indeed set all free!

In the mind of each one gathered, a vision of Earth appeared. At first there was a feeling of apprehension as the realities of the present came into clear focus: wars and pollution, greed and poverty, ignorance, cruelty and selfishness seemed to cover the surface of the land. Hardly anything could be seen clearly under the dark clouds, both astral and physical, that seemed to encroach upon all. Then, high above the miasma appeared the seven pairs of masters who had just addressed the incarnating souls from each of their retreats. A bright sun appeared above them and shone forth a ray of white light that refracted through their hearts as a rainbow of glory. The colored rays then descended upon the weary Earth, and along the light's path could be seen the souls that were descending to bring in a new day of hope and promise.

Gradually, the vision faded, and all were once again aware of their surroundings in their respective groups. After brief exchanges on how wonderful the session was, souls departed in small groups, each one absorbing the information, energy, and light received during this unforgettable farewell. At first, Narayan was so lost in thought that he did not notice whom he was with or where he was going, but after some time, he glanced up to notice he walked with old Baltar and the intriguing Sephira. "How do you feel about incarnating now, Narayan?" Baltar asked, even though the answer was obvious to all.

"With friends like those all around me, I have nothing to worry about. I'll play my part. If they do theirs, how can we lose?"

"Ahhh, forgetfulness, how easily does the soul forget once the clanging of matter drowns out the sensitive impressions of the inner. Even this great gathering will be soon forgotten to your incarnating conscious mind."

Sephira tried to counteract any dampening of Narayan's ebullient mood, "Oh Baltar, certainly we will seek to remind Narayan if his memory should in any way falter."

Narayan, a bit embarrassed, yet greatly pleased at her esteem of him, calmly remarked, "Oh, don't worry about me. How could I ever forget such a transcendent experience? I will treasure it always and hearken back to it often if my feet stray from my inner vision... Ah yes, the jewel of the heart, surely I will not lose hope as long as I can retain the perspective gained in this cycle of inner preparation."

Baltar quipped with a laugh, "While we can hope that you will remember it all, the cup of forgetfulness must be drunk by all entering through the veil. Where would the drama be if the end of the story was known?"

Then in a serious tone he remarked, "The time to enter

more fully into the womb of your mother is coming soon. The planets are in their stations; the angles and degrees are set for your descent. Prepare yourself, son, in the deepest meditation upon your Holy Presence that you can muster. Review your plans deeply. Remember our faces and your vows.

"Here we are at the re-entry chambers—the border between our realm and Earth. You are already adjusting to your embryonic form at an unconscious level. Later in the gestation process, you will be expected to be more present in the womb, but even then, there will be long periods of sleep when you will be awake again here in the retreats, and we will have more time to discuss our joint projects in greater detail. We love you, my boy, and many are counting on you. We must briefly leave you here with those who are adept at managing these points of embarkation and who will help you and your mother in the formation of your physical vehicle."

CHAPTER 12

The Previewing Chamber

Narayan walked down a long hallway, down some stairs and was amazed at what he saw when he opened the door. There was a room with five screens and two masters. They greeted him at the door and warmly welcomed him. The male being, Marshall, bowed deeply and said, "We have timed your conception with a great degree of accuracy and now you have arrived at the exact moment of gestation when you are needed."

The feminine being, Minerva, with curly hair in a loose afro, tapping on a console and gazing at the screen above her. "Auspicious timing," she declared as Marshall patted Narayan on the back, bringing his awareness back to the room. "An energetic umbilical cord is now established between your soul and the developing embryo, thus imprinting your vibration, consciousness and karma onto your new body. Later, you'll be expected to spend more time floating about in the womb, and your mom will experience your entrance as *the quickening*, when your mother with feel the first fluttering of your life within her."

Narayan could feel inside of himself the cells dividing and multiplying, even while he watched it on the screen. By focusing his attention, he could zoom in and see the chromosomes lining up in the process of mitosis.

"Amazing, isn't it?" breathed Minerva. "We never get bored of watching the intelligence of the Holy Spirit and the wondrous designs of Elohim, the cosmic creators, in action."

Then Narayan noticed the two other screens to his left. The upper one had what looked somewhat like a beehive, with dots moving around and lining up at the various cells.

Marshall explained, "That is the outline of this section of

this retreat, delineating the thousands of conception and gestation rooms that we utilize. There is quite a backlog of requests for re-entry, as you can see. You are fortunate to be getting such a good opportunity at this time."

Minerva pointed to the lower screen, "This one has a map of the Earth with details on all the prospective parents. Unfortunately, many of those conceiving children at this time are the ones least capable of meeting their physical, let alone their emotional and spiritual needs."

Marshall added, "But as you can see, there is such a waiting list that many would rather be born in a refugee camp in North Africa than be out of embodiment where there is little that they can do to balance their karma or repay their debts to life."

Narayan queried, "Why don't they just wait for a better opportunity?"

Minerva answered, "There are about twenty billion souls associated with Earth and many of them want to be on Earth during this transition from Pisces to Aquarius. We don't want to see the piled-up karma from the last 2000 years being pushed ahead to the next cycle."

Narayan commented, "So you are saying that because there are so many difficulties and so much suffering available on Earth, that billions of souls want to be incarnated to experience that?"

Marshall answered, "Well, basically, yes. Pleasure is not top on the list of why souls want to reincarnate. We have much higher and more refined pleasures up here, but we don't have many ways for people to balance the debts that they made while in the physical. That is where they must go to balance the ledger. Plus, many want to play their roles in helping to bring in the New Day on Earth."

They turned away from the screen that was portraying Narayan's little embryo.

Narayan commented, "I have found in those screens something I have long desired."

"What? A new body?"

"No, a womb with a view!"

With a hearty laugh, they both put a hand on his shoulder and Minerva said, "You may go now, but be aware that there will be times when you feel tired and need to lie down in this retreat. This is when you will be more conscious of your new life in the womb."

Marshall continued, "It's normal to feel emotional, to feel like crying or laughing. This is a sign you are integrating with your new body."

Narayan thanked them for helping with his new incarnation and left the room with a deep sense of gratitude for all those servants in the higher realms who are working so hard to bring in those souls who have a role to play in the healing and transformation of the Earth.

CHAPTER 13

Cosmic Education & Psychology

Patiently waiting outside in the hallway, Narayan found Sephira and said, "Greetings, dear one!"

"You can call me Lila now. That is the name my parents are to give me. I want to get used to it.

"Sure thing, *Saph-Lila!*"

"Okay, but seriously, Narayan, we need time together to learn of each other's missions so we can be sure to keep each other on track."

"Please, Lila, I'm really curious about what you have been studying."

"It has been so exciting, I have been studying with three newly ascended masters who just graduated from Earth this past century."

"Well, who are they?"

Well, on Earth, they were known as Maria Montessori, JRR Tolkien, and Carl Jung."

"Wow, that is quite an eclectic course of study. What is the connection between them and your mission?"

Lila paused for a few moments to put her thoughts together then answered, "I am to teach parents and teachers how to raise children and youth so as to keep them connected to their heart, soul and spirit."

"That's perfect," declared Narayan, "for I am to practice and teach the healing of the heart and soul as well! I have heard of Maria Montessori's schools, but don't really know much about her teaching."

"She is a genius. She was the first female medical doctor in Italy. She took the poor children who seemed hopeless and used her pedagogical methods on them. They ended up outscoring the wealthy and intelligent kids on standardized tests."

"How did she ever manage to do it?"

"She trusted in the inner wisdom of the child. She created an enriched, child-friendly environment and gave the right lessons at the right time. The children absorbed just what they needed, as the teaching was individualized for each of them. Instead of teachers, she called the adults *guides,* whose job it was to attune to the inner guide or higher self of the child. She postulated that each child's mind was absorbent and that there were sensitive periods when the brain was more open to certain information."

"So, in a practical way, how does that differ from a regular classroom?"

"Well, the guide will gather a few children around her and present a lesson, let's say, counting with beads and then tell the children that now they know how to do the work with the beads they can take out this lesson and repeat it whenever and however often they want to. So, let's say a child's brain is now ready for learning letters. In a regular class, they may teach everyone about numbers or history at the same time, but here the child can choose whatever she feels interested in, perhaps taking out and tracing the sandpaper letters over and over again, while another classmate may feel led to work on bead counting. All the lessons are at the child's level and pace, with child-sized seats and desks so they can get down to the business of doing what she called *the work* of building themselves."

"Isn't it total chaos to have a room full of children each doing their own thing?"

"You'd be amazed! The guide makes sure the children are well rounded and cover all the topics, but the children take out their work, do it as long as they like, and then neatly put it back on the shelves. Another difference is that three grades are in one class, so a child can accelerate as fast as they want and not be held back by the group and the older children assist the younger ones, which builds a sense of community."

Narayan asked, "Did she mention if she was pleased with the way her method was being applied in the Montessori schools of today?"

"Well, she did say a few things. One was that she envisioned the teens living in an agrarian farm environment, living close to the land and learning practical skills. There are only a few schools that have implemented this. With the prevalence of electronics everywhere, she would like to see more kids being unplugged from them and instead plugged into the Holy Spirit, which can best be found living with nature. Another thing she wrote about that hasn't really been implemented was the idea of *the atrium*."

"What's that?"

"She envisioned a special, small, quiet room where a child could retreat for contemplation, meditation or prayer. She understands the need for separation of church and state, but that does not mean that spirituality should be taken out of the children's lives, just not a specific religious dogma taught in school."

"The last thing she mentioned is that there must always be progress. She taught on Earth one hundred years ago. There has been much research on education, brain and emotional development since then. She is particularly interested in what has been called "right-brain education." This new understanding shows that, especially in the first six years of life, the brain is capable of absorbing incredible amounts of information. Rapidly showing flash cards on many topics is one way to download encyclopedic amounts of information into the subconscious. She feels that using music, movement and play helps learning much more than sitting in desks all day. Children can even learn ESP and clairvoyance through games. There are also movements, like Brain Gym, that balance the hemispheres of the brain and lead to more effective learning. These exercises are being used to counteract much of the ADD symptoms seen in modern children."

"Wait a minute. What kind of games teach ESP?"

"Montessori said that Japanese researchers have found that you can use any objects, like colored magic markers, plastic animals or toy cars. Let's say you have two toy fire trucks, two ambulances and two police cars. You give the child one of each and you hide yours and put one of them under a blanket and visualize sending a mental image of the hidden vehicle to the child. Then the child touches the one that he thinks it is. It's amazing that after a while, a child can guess it right every time, as long as they are relaxed and go with what comes to mind first."

Narayan thought about all of this for some moments and then asked, "So how do you think her teaching is related to my mission of becoming a healer of the soul?"

"It is a perfect match! She is speaking of the education of the heart and soul—the whole person. The child must be well balanced and happy, including eating a natural-foods diet, which they learn how to prepare as they mature. The parents and guides must tune into the strengths and weaknesses of the child and help their students to develop their full potential and discover what they are truly passionate about, for that will lead them to their missions and careers."

Just then, they heard a high-pitched tone in their inner ear, like the ringing of a bell and received a telepathic message saying that they were to come to the Advanced Psychology Auditorium to attend a class taught by Carl Jung and JRR Tolkien.

"How is that for timing?" exclaimed Narayan.

"It's truly amazing! That's exactly what I was going to

discuss next, but they have never taught together before, as far as I know."

Narayan added, "I think Jung had taught about meaningful coincidences—what he called synchronicity—while on Earth. Now he must be a master of them in Heaven."

Soon they made their way to a beautiful alabaster building with giant columns along the front. Apparently, many others had received the message as well. Hundreds of students were making their way to the assembly.

After everyone was settled, Jung spoke first, "I am grateful that so many of you are interested in our discussion on psychology and archetypes. People really want change, and if they knew better, they would do better—but without an understanding of the quest that each soul is on, they will never make sense of the vicissitudes of life. I myself have learned a lot since I have been here. Knowing the laws of karma and reincarnation, knowing of the chakras and the functioning of the subtle bodies, and reading the Akashic Records has helped further my understanding of the psyche and the soul."

Tolkien added, "Myths and legends have been the main avenue for teaching of the soul for thousands of years. In modern times, we have the same archetypes in new forms, whether it is the Land of Oz, Star Wars, the Lord of the Rings, the Grail Quest or the epic stories contained in the Bible, the soul learns of its eternal drama through the sparking of the imagination in stories."

Jung chimed in: "The King, the Dragon, the Princess, the Sacred Sword, the Jewel, the Sacred Flame, the Witch, the Serpent…" These are all powerfully charged images that pervade the subconscious mind. Dreams are one way the deeper reality of the soul is conveyed to the outer personality. We know that everything in the physical world is made of cosmic dust, the explosion of ancient stars and galaxies and the thoughtforms of the soul that mold it all into physical reality. People project what is within them onto the plastic substance of the "outer world" and it becomes their reality. It is easy for people to agree that their dreams may be their subconscious projections, but quite a leap to suggest the outer world itself is but the precipitation of thought and feeling into a seemingly 'real' form. Just because we all agree on a consensus reality, doesn't mean that it is ultimately true.

"There are two ways to see the world: as an inner reality that expresses itself outwardly, or an outer reality that produces inner experience. But the brain is not the soul. We in this room dwell in the realm of what those on Earth call 'Heaven.' We have a mind and we vibrate at a higher frequency than those of Earth, but we have no biological brain. We operate from our etheric brain, upon which the physical brain is precipitated into form. Anyway, my brainless friends, we must reawaken the people of Earth to their destiny on the path of the Hero, which is the path of every soul from God—back to God."

Tolkien then spoke up: "Consider any story that people repeat for generations, in that case you can know that there is something deeper, there is something that touches their soul and speaks to them in universal archetypes. Take my books as an example. Frodo is a hobbit. He is from a small folk with big hairy feet who loves the creature comforts of food, drink and smoke. But within him is the image of the Hero upon whom the salvation of his people and indeed the world depends. Each soul must know that the battle of Light and Darkness first begins within the Self. Then there is the outer battle that must be waged that demands the fellowship of all. In my tale, I symbolized the combined harmonious action of these different beings as elves, dwarfs, men and wizards. In reality, there is a cooperation among the angels, elementals, human souls and masters, which these mythological beings symbolize."

Jung spoke up again: "The role of parents is so ultimately powerful that the child's image of the Father/Mother God itself will be colored deeply by their relationship with their Earthly parents in early life. Is the father the wise king guiding with wisdom, or the despotic ruler that breaks the will of the child? Is the mother the wise fairy godmother who comforts and guides the heart, or the wicked witch that uses her spells of condemnation and guilt to control the free will of the soul?"

Tolkien added: "The orphan is a common archetype in children's stories. There are the orphans Annie and Oliver, Heidi, Hansel and Gretel, Cinderella, and Dorothy, even the motherless Nemo the clownfish, Ariel, the Little Mermaid, Luke Skywalker the Jedi Knight, and Simba the young Lion King. Every child knows the broken heart of the fatherless Bambi. It appears that a message is being sent to the soul of the child that Earth is not their real home and those who rear them are not their eternal parents. In these stories, not only is the early environment found to be difficult, it is often downright hostile and evil."

Jung chimed in again: "That severe challenge sparks a quest in the soul to find the path to what I have termed *individuation*. Finding who is *The I AM in Me*—the individual God Identity—that is separate from all the influences of the environment. What is the source of my life? How can I get back to that fount of reality? Ease and pleasure have no part in these adventure stories... Becoming whole is difficult. It is a struggle and a battle. Although the world may tempt the Hero with values that are the antithesis of the soul's true principles, the role of parents in instilling these cosmic tenets cannot be overestimated.

"If parents were to work on their souls, their psychology and their spirituality to the extent that they outpicture the virtues of the higher planes, they could more easily represent the Father/Mother God to the soul of the child. To know the true laws of life from an early age enables the growing child and thus the adult to make the right decisions that enable them to accomplish the unique mission for which they incarnated."

Tolkien spoke again: "The archetypes of the astrological signs are an infinite study in themselves—the twelve lines on the clock, the twelve months of the year, the twelve signs of the zodiac. Each one has a unique frequency, vibration and quality. The

Greeks and all ancient civilizations studied the stars and took care in mapping out the year by the zodiac. The stories of the Odyssey or the Labors of Hercules tell of the soul needing to pass the initiations on each line of the cosmic clock. Each sign has a positive and negative potential and it requires the ingenuity of the soul to learn how to transmute the negative propensities into positive virtues."

Jung quipped: "Did you know that the archetypal Book of Revelations in the Bible mentions one of the crosses of astrology? It is the mention of the man, the calf, the lion, and the flying eagle. These correspond to Aquarius, Taurus, Leo, and Scorpio. Mystically, these four fixed points have to do with the qualities of service, sacrifice, surrender and selflessness. These are always the tests given to the advanced souls to see if they are ready to transcend to the next level. When these tests are successfully passed the individual is ready to receive more light and opportunity."

"Carl, may I continue?" asked Tolkien.

"Certainly, brother J. R. R. R. R.!" Everyone laughed.

"Anyway, these little planets have such an exacting effect on life that it is no wonder that many astrologers speculate if indeed there is such a thing as free will. It is the individualized Hero that is truly free, but much of humanity is governed almost exclusively by the fates written in their stars. These planets have all had some sort of life evolving on them—a few physical, others

astral, and others mental. The energetic records of these evolutions to some extent determine the frequency and vibration of the planet thus inhabited.

"The Mercurians were predominantly mental and scientific, excelling in language and books. The Venusians were great lovers of art and music, beauty and romance. The Martians tended toward regimentation, action and conflict. So, as these planets come into certain angles, their energies either harmonize or conflict with each other. Sixty or one-hundred-and-twenty-degree angles (sextiles and trines) bring positive and harmonious energy and ninety or one-hundred-and-eighty-degree angles (squares or oppositions) bring more negative or challenging energy.

The everchanging influences of the frequencies of these planets impinge on the emotional, mental and physical bodies through the chakras and glands, creating much of the experience of the individual. Thus, a good astrologer can tell by the archetypal language of astrology what the psychological makeup is of an individual, what their quest is, what the best timing for action is, and in general, what the expected energy forecast is so that the soul can prepare for eventualities ahead of time."

Jung added: "There is a very recent situation on Earth that is concerning to us... and that is the presence of hundreds of satellites presently orbiting the Earth. They are beaming frequencies, vibrations, sounds and images into the subconscious mind and subtle bodies of the residents of Earth. It creates a din that blots out the deep peace that is radiated from the stars in space. Through the entertainment media, there are horror movies, stories of sexual infidelity and perversion, images of wars, and all manner of distortions beamed from these satellites. They are first and foremost irritators of the nervous system on the physical level. Until this space junk can be removed from the Earth's aura, there will come forth, and already there is some, technology that can protect the auric field from this electromagnetic pollution."

The high-pitched tone rang out and everyone sighed the same complaint, *"Awwwww!"*

Tolkien ended, "Yes, that is the end our class. Maybe we should continue to teach together, Carl?"

To which there was a thunderous and sustained applause.

"We understand that all of you are on the fast-track of self-knowledge and are all planning to descend into a new birth soon. When I wrote my book, *The Silmarillion*, I wrote a creation story of my own universe. Little do most know in their outer self that we are all creators. We create our little microcosm and people it with the thoughts and feelings of our soul. One day we will be-come creators in the macrocosmic sense and create our own plan-ets, stars and solar systems. My fellow students—remember to respect the gods, but know that they all serve the one God within your Heart."

With that, they both bowed low and while holding each other's hand, simply disappeared.

CHAPTER 14

An Invitation to the Lower Strata

N arayan and Lila sat in deep silence for a while, held hands, and got up to leave. Lila asked, "Well, how did you enjoy the teaching?"

Narayan answered, "It was so interesting and different from the college classes I recall from Earth. It was truly astonishing. When he was naming the different stories about the various orphans, I could see the entire story, like I had absorbed a whole movie in a flash."

Lila responded, "Oh, yes. We call that downloading. An entire book or movie or concept can be imparted to another, from mind to mind. Even on Earth, it's possible to attune to the consciousness of a teacher, author or master and absorb information instantly from their higher mental body."

As they walked, Lila pointed up as she noticed something blue descending from above.

"Look up there!" Lila exclaimed.

"It looks like a ball of lightning!" Narayan declared.

"But I can make out a form in the center," Lila added.

"It's coming right toward us!"

Then, a beautiful angel clothed in armor of electric-blue light descended slowly.

"Hail, Children of the Most High God. I send greetings from the Archangels, whom I serve!" declared the angel.

"And who are you?" asked Narayan.

"I am Shamariel, a blue-lightning angel. I summon you to embark with me on a journey into the lower strata of life."

"What would be our purpose there?" inquired Narayan.

"Look this way, and behold my projection screen." At that, he plunged his blue flame sword into the ground and balanced his shield against it. Soon the shield lit up and projected a three-dimensional image that seemed to float in the air in front of them.

"This will show, in a holographic movie, which will soon be the preferred method of communication and entertainment on Earth, a scene of karma that you, Narayan, had created in a previous life.

Narayan immediately recognized himself as the man who was being entreated by a passionate and emotional teenager.

"Please, I know you are my father... just recognize me as your son. Then they will let me enter the university and I will be able to make an honest living. But without education, I am bound for poverty," he cried as he grabbed the man's feet, tears falling on the man's toes.

Narayan watched in trepidation as he saw the man who he had been step back and say, "Indeed, you are of my body, as the scullery maid who was my servant has told you, but I cannot recognize you publicly, as that will threaten my own standing with my wife, whose inheritance has financed my lifestyle, and that of my legitimate heirs, who depend upon me."

The scene changed as this young man's soul was followed throughout the centuries, descending into alcoholism, drug abuse, debauchery, gambling and crime.

"You see," Shamariel spoke gently, "that scene was a turning point for this soul, who has in turn affected many other souls in a distinctly negative way. If you can turn him toward the Light, then he may, in turn, direct others toward the Light and thus earn their freedom."

"How can I find him?"

"First, I must charge your aura with an aura of protection," Shamariel replied. "This is something we do daily in the ritual for the recharging of the angels."

"Is it like recharging a battery?" quipped Narayan.

Shamariel smiled as he replied "In a way, yes. You see, angels descend from a high etheric level and are not native to the physical or astral planes. In their normal evolution, other than in service to mankind, they would have no business there. But since there is such a need for our assistance, if we are invited by someone from these lower planes, then that free will opens the doorway whereby we may enter and intercede."

"There needs to be a formal invitation?" asked Narayan.

"A specific prayer is often answered very specifically; however, even *God help me!* is enough for us to render assistance."

"So, if I was, let's say, about to get into a car accident and called out, *Angels of God, help me!* then you would come?"

"Instantaneously! We have been known to rearrange time and space so that an onlooker would swear that a miracle occurred—that the car seemed to be lifted in the air over the truck and set down in a field, for instance."

"Wow, I have heard such stories. To witness something like that must really strengthen one's faith."

"Blessed are they who believe and yet have not seen," Shamariel said.

He closed his eyes for a moment, as he was doing some searching on the inner planes, then he stated, "I will take to you him, your illegitimate son in a former lifetime. He is in a lower level of the astral plane. We will put on your protection now. Visualize armor around you, made of intense blue-flame power."

Narayan looked down and was amazed that he could actually see blue armor forming all around him.

Shamariel continued, "Good, now visualize a giant, golden disc over your solar plexus—we call this the Great Sun Disc. Very good, periodically keep this visualization going if you feel the lower vibrations are attacking you."

"Are we going to be under attack?" asked Narayan.

"Have faith. I will be by your side the entire time. Now, understand, we are going to be in a dimension that is more dense and more illusory. It will seem like a waking dream. Anything you can imagine can become a reality there."

"So, anyone can do anything there, like fly at will?" Narayan asked in amazement.

"Theoretically, the only problem is that anyone who enters the lower astral plane is, in some way, asleep in their dream. They think it is all real. But since you are coming from a higher level, and since I will be overshadowing you, you will be more awake in your dream, more alert and aware, and less susceptible to the limitations and the illusions that they all accept as real, while there."

"Is that how Jesus and the saints performed their miracles?"

"This is an apt comparison, but not quite. The people dwelling on Earth are dwelling in *maya*, or illusion, yes. However, the lower astral plane, known as purgatory to those in traditional religion, is steeped even further in darkness, and the illusions of one's own making based on one's karma. It is true that Jesus and the other avatars came to Earth fully awakened, losing almost nothing from their high estate and communion with their Presence. These avatars could bend the natural laws that seem so rigid to those who are asleep on the lower planes. Anything they could visualize or imagine, with full faith in their feeling world and that was according to the Will of God, they could manifest as reality."

"This ought to be fun... Let's go!"

"Hold on, my friend. You will not be an adept in the Laws of Precipitation just by entering the lower planes... Another sobering thought is that even Jesus did not convince everyone of the truth of their being, when they witnessed miracles upon miracles. So, no guarantees—just be sincere and try your best. This is a rescue mission for a dear soul with whom you are karmically tied. I recall a case where I appeared to someone who had left embodiment, but due to their heavy karma, was stuck in a dreadful place in the lower astral plane. I appeared to this soul in full glory and power, but by free will, the soul refused to come up higher with me. However, when a familiar friend gently suggested they leave the old ways behind, they agreed to be escorted to the octaves of light."

Narayan replied, "Well, if I'm ever in a pinch, I'll be sure that I call upon you, Shamariel. I will gladly accept your assistance with full faith."

"Thus, let us embark!"

CHAPTER 15

A Card Game in Hell

At that, Shamariel put his hand on Narayan's shoulder and said, "Just close your eyes and visualize the soul you had rejected so long ago and stay focused on him."

Narayan had the sense of rushing through the air. Soon the atmosphere felt denser, like moving through water, then Shamariel let go and said, "We come to the lower astral plane when necessity demands it, but it is NOT where we like to, as they say, *hang out.*"

Narayan opened his eyes and saw what looked like an alley in a major metropolitan area. There was garbage everywhere, with rats scurrying around and the place reeked with a musty, dank odor.

"Let us enter incognito," Shamariel said. He handed Narayan a beige trench coat and they both covered up their glowing blue armor. "And don't worry; I have your back," he winked as he pulled aside his coat and showed Narayan the hilt of his blue flame sword he carried on his waist. "The soul we seek is currently named Al. He has been dead and wandering the lower planes for ten years now. He has lost almost all sense of home. Remember, we are here to free his soul."

They both smiled as Shamariel yelled in a deep voice, "Open up! We want to play!"

As soon as the door opened, Narayan had the urge to retrace his steps and get out of there. And then he realized that this was hell—or at least purgatory. But, one look from the angel strengthened his resolve.

Scuzzy is the one word that came to Narayan's mind. Beer bottles everywhere, moldy food, scurrying rodents, and what looked like dense shadows hovering around the three men sitting at the card table.

"You guys ready to ante up?" Al asked with a tough-guy attitude.

"I'll watch, he'll play," Shamariel answered.

"Oh, a goody two-shoes, are you?" teased Al.

"Well, let's say I trust more in faith than luck," Shamariel responded.

"I have faith, too—faith in cold, hard money. That's all you can depend on," Al responded in a gruff voice.

At that, Shamariel produced a pouch of tinkling silver coins and handed it to Narayan.

"I'm sorry, we haven't been properly introduced. I'm Nar... I mean, Nathan, and this is my friend, *uh*... Sam," Narayan stammered.

"A talkative one, huh? Well, Nate and Sam, I'm Al, this is Fred, and that there is Jake. It's Five Card Draw."

Al dealt the cards and threw a silver coin in the middle of the table. Narayan loosened the pouch and did likewise.

Narayan asked, "You guys been playing for a while?"

To which, Jake responded, "More betting, less talking!"

Fred, seeing that Nathan felt cut short, added, "Be nice to the kid; he just got here. Hey Nate, wanna smoke?"

Narayan looked at Shamariel, who gave a slight nod.

Narayan simply said, "Don't mind if I do." Then, he closed his eyes and concentrated. Smoke started wafting out from the skin of his entire body.

Fred and Jake's jaws dropped and their eyes widened. Al just stared, but then put on his tough-guy face and said, "Oh, yeah, I saw a trick like that in Vegas. Come on, let's get on with the game. I'll bet two and take two cards. Fred and Jake did likewise, while shaking their heads in disbelief.

Narayan threw in two coins and said, "I'll take one."

Al, keeping his poker face on, tossed in three more coins, so did Fred, but Jake folded. After Narayan added his three coins, it was showdown time.

Al broke into a big smile with his crooked and yellow-stained teeth and said, "Beat that, boys!" And laid out his hand of five hearts.

Narayan congratulating him saying, "Oh, Al, you are all heart... nice flush!" ,Remembering that the laws of nature could be bent down here, he held out his right hand and moved his fingers down as if depressing a lever. They all distinctly heard the sound of a toilet flushing.

Fred stood up and looked around, as Jake looked under the table. Al looked at Narayan and said, "Okay, so you're a Vegas-style magician and a sound-effects guy as well?"

Narayan, ignoring their reactions, asked Al, "If you ever get tired of this place and want to travel, I know a great place you would..."

Al cut him off, "No, I'm happy here—I have everything I could want..."

Narayan cut in, "What about college? Didn't you ever want to achieve something more in your life?"

Al stood up, "I'm here to play poker, not talk about college! I think you guys have outworn your welcome. Time to go!"

Narayan didn't budge, "I think I hit a sore spot there... You did have dreams when you were younger, didn't you?"

Al, who was visibly shaken and angry, said with a slight quiver in his voice, , "I think you'd best be going, and right now. I mean it."

Narayan pulled out a card he thought would work, "What's the matter, Al? Are you afraid of death? Well, I'll break it to you - you've been dead for a decade."

Shamariel just shook his head and whispered, "that almost never works."

Al just stared at him, "What do you mean, dead? I'm breathing, ain't I? I just played cards. I just had a drink. You want to talk about being dead? Well, I can arrange that for you, buddy!"

Shamariel, forgotten by everyone, spoke next, "Your father wouldn't let you go to the university. That was the turning point, wasn't it?

Al said in a pained and raspy voice, "He hated me!"

With that Shamariel reached out and touched Al in the center of his forehead. Narayan transformed before Al's eyes into the exact form he wore when Narayan was Al's father all those centuries ago.

He looked lovingly into Al's eyes and spoke directly to his soul, "My son, please forgive me for abandoning you. It was a grave mistake on my part. If you can trust me now, come with me. I will take you to a school that is wonderful beyond your wildest dreams."

Al had a visible expression of shock, and managed to stammer, "I...I think I remember you...from a long time ago..."

Narayan put his hand on his shoulder, "Al, I recognize you now as my heir and welcome you back into my family."

Al could hardly speak, but managed to say, "Back then...I didn't feel worthy to even be called your son...I was in so much pain..."

Narayan, whose turn it was to shed a tear, said, "This son of mine was dead and is alive again; he was lost and now has been found."

Al softened as the weight of many years fell off him. He became transfigured. A robe of white light replaced his worn-out, shabby garments. His face became younger and he appeared as a teenager. He looked over to Shamariel, who assumed his regular form, complete with blue-flame armor.

Fred managed to stammer, "Does... this mean we won't be finishing our game?"

To which Jake whispered with a hiss, "Shhh, he left his bag of silver on the table."

Narayan looked at them and said, "Keep the change boys. Al will keep *his change!*"

Shamariel added, "I am Shamariel, an angel of protection and deliverance from the upper etheric planes, what you know as Heaven. We have come to free Al from his bondage and to reunite him with his father from the past, whose name is Narayan. Fred and Jake, if you pray often to find the higher way, one day, I may be back to escort you two as well to a much better place."

Al looked to them, "Well, old buds, looks like I'm going... I'll try to send you a message on how I'm doing up there. He gave them both a hug. Fred and Jake were shaken, as if waking from a dream.

Narayan lifted his sword and exclaimed, "The Light of God never fails!" With that statement, the entire room was cleansed of all negative entities. All the grime and vermin disappeared, and the room sparkled.

Then, Shamariel enfolded Narayan and Al in his wings of light and with an explosion of light, they were gone.

They reappeared in a beautiful room of a large retreat on

the second level of the etheric plane. Al stood in shock for a minute and looked at the ornately carved marble walls and sat down on the large comfortable bed.

"So, I am really dead, huh?" he sighed.

Shamariel answered, "It has been ten Earth years since you left your physical body, and finally, the right moment came when you could be set free."

"Will I now stand in some kind of Judgment Hall to be told all about the mistakes I made?"

"In a way, yes, but you will be your own judge and some wise counselors will help you to set up a new set of circumstances, so you can grow and learn. When you are ready and fully prepared, you will enter into another round of incarnation. Fear not, Al. It has all been for your benefit."

Narayan added, "If you have any metaphysical debts toward anyone, you will be given opportunities to pay them back, just as me coming to rescue you was a blessing given to me to help me balance my debt to you."

Al said, "Thank you! I'm so excited to start learning, but I feel so tired."

Shamariel bid Al to lie down and said, "Rest and sleep. You will soon become more accustomed to this dimension."

"But I'm scared to dream. I hurt a lot of people, you see. Even though I'm in this Heaven now, I still feel bad for what I've done."

Three angels then entered the room. "We will remove your guilt and shame from your energy field." The first angel whispered in a half singing voice as they showered him with flower petals and anointed his forehead with aromatic oil. He lay back on the bed and didn't fight their ministrations.

He was almost asleep, but then he roused himself, saying,

"Wait! What about my father in this last life? Where is he? He must be in hell."

Shamariel answered, "He is in the Earth, in a new physical body. He is eight years old. He has a metaphorical gold nugget in his soul and will begin to shine in this life."

"The only shine I ever saw in him was moonshine."

"Yes, he earned the karma of being born to alcoholic parents, but by grace, his mother was able to quit before pregnancy. He has in his life-plan to become an Alcoholics Anonymous counselor and will lead many to sobriety and self-knowledge."

"Wow, reincarnation is true, then, huh? Well, I guess God is merciful, thank God!"

With that he lay down and drifted off to sleep.

"So, what now? Will he just sleep?" asked Narayan.

One of the attending angels whispered, "This deep sleep is very restorative to the soul. After a time, he will be in a state of consciousness called *devachan*."

"What is that?" Narayan queried.

The second angel responded, "It is a state of being that is intermediate between two Earthly lives for the purpose of soul healing. It is an almost completely subjective world where one projects and lives out one's hopes and unfulfilled soul desires."

The third angel touched Al's forehead and after a brief time said, "He will see himself attending a prestigious university and studying hard and getting good grades. This seems to be a long pent-up desire that he wants to experience."

"What does it mean, almost completely subjective?" Narayan asked.

The angel answered, "It means that someone, even you, could enter into his dream world and play a part and experience his inwardly projected world. You could be a fellow student or professor and interact with his soul. Maybe later you can come back and do just that."

"That would be very interesting. I would like to do that, especially if there is any remaining karma that we need to balance together."

The angel mentioned, "You can't really transform karma you made while in the physical while in devachan, but you can transform tendencies and habits that will come in very handy in the next embodiment."

CHAPTER 16

The Field of Dreams

The youth waited excitedly in the flower meadow, which was called the *Field of Dreams*. This name had a double meaning, for it was where children waiting to be born meet their prospective parents and discuss their hopes and dreams for their future—and it is also where the parents walk and talk with their future children while their bodies sleep in their beds at night. Narayan's higher self arranged for him to appear as the form he would be wearing in a few years on Earth.

A child watched in amazement as he saw tiny fairies balancing on the tips of flower petals as they played some sort of game. Then he heard from behind him, "Is that you, my child?"

"Of course it is, Stuart," Jennifer Landing said matter-of-factly to her husband, as she scooped up the child in her arms. The father tousled the boy's hair with a warm feeling in his heart.

"My name will be Harry!" the boy of about four years old said, with some surprise, as he had never remembered saying that name before.

Stuart sat down in the meadow and took his son into his lap, "Well, Harry, is there anything you want us to do in preparation for your birth?"

"Well, I love nature. So, anything you can do to find more happiness in nature would be good. And I love science—that's part of the reason why I chose you as my dad. And I love God!"

"So, you want me to find the connection between nature, science and spirituality?"

"If you want me to be happy, that would be a great start, daddy."

"And what about me?" asked the mother. "What can I do to make you feel more welcome?"

"Well, mommy, can you just become really healthy, please? Also, can it not just be your body, but also in your feelings and your mind? Then, while I am in your womb, you will create the best possible body for me. Find out who you really are, then you can guide me in doing the same."

"You are a wise little boy!" she said in awe.

Beep, Beep, Beep!

Stuart Landing reached over his wife to hit the snooze button. Then he whispered to his wife, "I had a dream that I was with you and a baby ... and he said something to me, but I don't recall what it was.

"I don't remember anything from my dream either, but I was just thinking about our future child as the alarm went off... Stu, I think it's a boy."

Stuart had a new feeling of exhilaration as he went about his day. He had a little time before his class started. He was a professor of theoretical physics at the local university. It was a clear and brisk fall day. Everything seemed so alive. He admired the sky and the trees and enjoyed the crunching sound of leaves beneath his feet. Millions of dried chlorophyll factories, done with their job of creating sugar out of dirt, air and sunlight... amazing, he thought. He felt the warm sunshine on his face. Those photons were hurled from a thermo-nuclear reaction from a star a mere seven-to-eight minutes ago, he mused, and after hitting my skin they produced a hormone in my body, which we call vitamin D, that is boosting my immunity and preventing cancer, plus dozens of other effects.

For the first time in his life, Stuart really thought about experiencing gravity and imagined the Earth hurtling around the sun at thousands of miles per hour for billions of years. And he felt the sphere of the Earth under his feet, imagining that he was as likely on the bottom of the Earth, as much as on the top of it. So, he jumped, imagining himself under the Earth and being pulled back again by gravity. He laughed, feeling a little giddy, as if he were a child again.

He looked up at the giant oaks and suddenly he remembered the movie, *Horton Hears a Who*, which he had seen with his other children some years ago. These trees are like blades of grass and he is like an ant. Suddenly, his perspective changed and he could see all the planets circling the sun, and the sun whirling around the galaxy, and billions of galaxies expanding in the universe, each consisting of billions of stars. He walked back to his car, thinking of new ways to inspire his students to really see the wonder of the universe through science.

Jennifer's day wasn't starting out very well. She had that strange feeling that you get when you know you had a dream but can't quite get at it, knowing that the memories of the dream could all come back in a moment. But, that moment never came. Instead, she felt irritable. She looked at herself in the mirror and thought how ugly she looked without her makeup. Something was missing in her life, and not knowing what it was made her feel depressed.

After a few weeks, Stuart started to become concerned about his wife. He tried to share his new realizations about the universe with her, thinking it would lift her spirits, but she thought he was getting rather weird and a little too 'out there.' When a surprise October snowstorm came, he showed her his book of snowflakes and asked her to see billions of these perfect individual crystals descending from the clouds. She just felt cold, said that soon it would all be dirty slush and the boys would be dragging that into the house. Stuart mentioned his concern for her again, and she finally agreed to seeing a doctor.

"Well, we have known about post-partum depression for decades. You know, the baby blues, but now we are getting into preventative medicine and are putting more and more pregnant women on anti-depressants," the doctor suggested.

"But won't that effect the baby's developing brain?"

"Well, I don't know for sure, but I think the benefits outweigh the risks. Look, you are becoming a mother, you should be happy. I'll write the prescription and you can fill it at your local pharmacy. And by the way, on the way out, make sure you get a flu shot."

"I heard they still have a derivative of mercury in those shots. I'm an older mom and I'm kind of worried about autism."

"Oh, nonsense! There have been thousands of reputable studies to debunk all those crazy Internet hoaxes. You don't want to become a crazy conspiracy theorist, do you?"

"Well...I'll think about it."

Think about it she did. Jennifer felt a knot in her stomach and a contracting feeling in her throat. She patted her growing belly and whispered, "I guess you are thinking what I'm thinking." She got out of there quickly, and a sigh of relief was heard in Heaven.

CHAPTER 17

A Demonic Affair

"**I**nkblot!" The demon yelled to his protégé, "You couldn't even get her to take one lousy heavy-metal-laden vaccine, which millions are just lining up for? We don't have too much info on this kid yet, but we know he's trouble. We can see the light increasing in her aura and we can tell he is some kind of healer. We found out the due date, ran the astrology and it seems like he has the potential to affect millions of people in a positive way. We can't allow that!"

"I tried. She usually listens to authority figures like this doctor, but this kid may have some sort of telepathic communication with her already."

"It seems the abortion idea didn't take, so if we can't kill or damage the kid, then it's on to plan B—divide and conquer!"

"You mean get the parents divorced?"

"Obviously! We recently made a new record of breaking up 50% of all marraiges, so I expect great results this time. Our techniques are getting more and more refined."

"I can scout out his workplace and see if there are any hot dames to tempt him."

"Speaking of hot, if you fail this time, I'll consider raking you over the coals again!" But in a friendlier tone he said, "Don't worry, I don't call you Inkblot for no reason."

"I thought it was because I was pure blackness, and amorphous as well."

"It's deeper than that. You see, in a Rorschach test, you are shown an inkblot and you free-associate. You project your inner images onto the stain. Someone might see angels, and another person, looking at the same blot, might see people having sex.

"I get it. I'm good at projecting images into unwitting people's subconscious minds."

"That's it. In that way, you easily manipulate desires."

"Wow, thanks for the reminder. I am great at that, and it's so fun to turn people to our side. It's so easy!"

"Yeah yeah, just don't let it get to your head. With all the advertisements and their subliminal messages, soon demon lackeys like you won't even be necessary. Just get the job done."

Inkblot was amazed how easy it was to get things rolling. Getting that cute new secretary Tiffany a seat right next to Stuart at the Science Department dinner party and arranging for Jennifer to decide not to attend was a cinch. Stuart normally didn't drink. But, his wife wasn't with him, and he felt a little shy about opening up to his colleagues at a social function. So, what harm could a few drinks do? Inkblot projected an olive into his subconscious and Stuart had a martini.

"Simple as that," Inkblot thought.

After he found the seating card with his name on it, Stuart greeted Tiffany with a handshake. They spoke about some things they had in common at work. It also came up that Tiffany was single and open to dating. Quite unexpectedly, Stuart found himself very attracted to this young woman. This is the first time he had seen her all dressed up, with her hair let down, and cleavage showing. There was a toast to the department and he had some wine, which somehow kept getting refilled right after it was drained. There was a rush in his head, and a light, flushed feeling throughout his body. He was very apologetic when the shrimp he had just dipped in some cocktail sauce slipped from his hand and made a spot on her dress right under her left breast. He instinctively put his napkin in some ice water and dabbed the spot before the stain could set. She laughed nervously as she unexpectedly found herself aroused by this sweet and gentle man.

Alarms started going off in Narayan's mind. At first, he couldn't fathom what the emergency was. He silenced his thinking, went into meditation and got the intuitive message that his father was in some sort of trouble, which was endangering his own divine plan. He immediately hurried to the nearest station of descent and soon found himself in the aura of his father. He was shocked to find him somewhat tipsy and his aura sending out feelers that were enwrapping the attractive young lady seated next to him. More astonishing was to see a little demon stationed below his belt, projecting images of sex scenes into his subconscious mind and lower chakras.

The demon was able to actually access every movie Stuart had ever seen where a guy meets a girl at a bar and then, in the next scene, they're naked in bed. Before Narayan realized what was happening, Stuart and Tiffany were going to his car and he was going to drive her home, as she had taken a cab to the party.

She wanted him to see how she had used *Feng Shui* to arrange her home. Things were moving too fast and Narayan realized he had to act quickly. Tiffany went to put some stain remover on her blouse and came back out in a bathrobe, with absolutely nothing on underneath!

Narayan instinctively shouted to the angels of God: *Help me, help me, help me!* Instantly, Shamariel the blue-flame angel appeared, complete with his blue-flame armor and sword. Narayan excitedly pointed at Inkblot busily manipulating Stuart's lower chakras. A lightning bolt streamed from the sword and a blue-and-white-fire surrounded the demon, pulling him from Stuart's aura and suspending him in the air.

"Good! Hold him there. We will deal with him later." Narayan said as he quickly started sending his own thoughtforms toward his father's third eye. As she led him by the hand toward the bedroom, Stuart felt like the trance he was in was suddenly lifted. He let go of her hand and looked at his wedding ring, which had never been removed since the day of his wedding. He recalled Jennifer putting it on his hand that day over 15 years earlier and remembered the vow before God and man that he affirmed by saying "I do." He then saw the image of Jennifer caressing her rounded belly as she was starting to show.

"I really have to be going, Tiffany," he stammered, as he quickly felt quite sober. "I feel more confident now about driving home on the freeway. Thanks for showing me your feng shui. Have a good night!" With that, he left and ran to his car.

"What are we going to do with this demon? I don't want him having another opportunity to split my family apart." The angel replied, "I'll keep him in this blue flame force-field, and you can reason with him. Get him to see the divine star of light deep within him. There is a chance of him being transformed."

Narayan approached the demon and asked him what he was trying to do to that man.

"Just following orders!"

"What happens if you fail?"

"Oh, no—you're the one who is incarnating in that family, aren't you! You're the one my master is afraid of!"

"Why are you working for an arch-demon when you could be serving the light?"

"Don't speak of the light! We are told that it will burn us and we will die from the light!"

"Are you more scared of the light, or of returning to your master with the failure of your mission?"

"Oh, woe is me—I have nowhere to go! He said he will torture me again for letting him down. I can't face him again."

"Then, face the star of light that I can dimly perceive in the center of your heart of darkness."

"What? I was never told about that."

"Just look deep within."

"Ahhh! It burns, it burns!" Suddenly, there was a brilliant flash of light all about him and there he stood, transformed into an angel of white light."

Then, Shamariel set him down on the floor and said, "See? That wasn't so bad! Look at you—you were originally an angel. You fell, through greed and selfishness and turned your light to darkness, until all that was left was that spark of light. You had been a therapist and a counselor who could help people clear subconscious images that kept them bound to bad habits. After you fell, you misused your knowledge to bind people to those same habits, draining the light off unsuspecting souls, which became food for you and your master, thus perpetuating evil on this planet."

"I am so sorry! How will I be punished?"

Shamariel responded, "Understanding your wrongs is enough punishment for now. I will bring you to Archangel Raphael. He will heal your memories and restore you to the service of the light where you can do penance for your misdeeds by serving in your original capacity. Perhaps, you can begin by healing this unfortunate young woman of her core shame and her subconscious memories of sexual abuse as a child."

"Not only that, I'm sure I could get some of my old cohorts to also be liberated. When we fell, we lost all memory of how merciful God is. We expected unending torture or eradication if we failed our demon master. I can also reveal to the angels how the dark ones plot and function."

Shamariel smiled and said, "That is all well and good, my angel, but all the plots of the lower ones are known to us. We practice forbearance because we see the divine spark in them and hold even them in the light of their future redemption."

131

Narayan could do nothing but praise the Lord for answering his calls, and for converting an enemy into an ally. He bid goodbye to Shamariel and invited this restored angel to assist him with his mission in his soul-therapy work.

CHAPTER 18

Inner Child Work

S tuart Landing couldn't sleep at all, not after what just almost happened. He had never been unfaithful to his wife, not even in his thoughts, and now this.

Jennifer was awake as well. He sat up, turned on the light and spilled the beans of his near disastrous experience. She put her arms around him and said that with the dark cloud she has been under, she could understand why he may be tempted by a more fun and attractive woman, but she was proud of his escape. They told each other they would forgive and forget. He affirmed his love for her and said he would gladly consecrate his vows to her again. He put his hand on her belly, visualized the tiny human growing in there, and vowed in his heart that nothing will tear his family apart. Finally, while cuddling together, they fell asleep.

When she awoke, she said, "Stuart, I have just dreamt that Rosaline told me to see her therapist. Maybe this depression is not just brain chemistry, but more psychological." She wasted no time and was able to get in to see Sophia the very next day.

Sophia, who was a psychotherapist with a spiritual nature, began, "Now, I am going to use a technique to help you access your subconscious mind. As I ask you questions, we are going to use a therapy called EMDR. As I move this light from side to side, just move your eyes and not your head. This will help balance the *Ha* that separates your left and right brain. Thus, material that you couldn't access with your conscious mind suddenly becomes available."

"I don't know how this can actually work, but I'm open," said Jennifer.

"Good. Now watch the light. Where did you sleep last night?"

"In my bed."

"Good, go back to your bed and go back to that morning when you had the dream about your baby."

"I'm seeing the child... It is a boy. Another boy. Oh, wow!"

"No, don't go there, that is the conscious mind. Go back to the dream."

"He is saying something to me, but I don't know what it is."

"Ask him to tell you again."

"He wants me to know one thing."

"What is that thing?"

"You are the one I have chosen to be my mother, but before you do, I need you to purify your body and mind and to find out who you really are!"

"That's it!"

"That's what?"

Sophia sighed, "That is why you have been depressed since that dream... you've got some work to do and you don't know who you really are."

"That's silly. I'm Jennifer Landing. I've been on this Earth for 38 years. I have a good memory of all my experiences since early childhood."

Sophia continued, "This is not about your personality. It's deeper than that. It is a question of your soul. It is a spiritual quest you must be engaged in. Who are you in the eternal sense of being? Who were you before you were born? Who will you be after you die?

"How am I supposed to find out those kinds of answers?

Nobody can actually know those kinds of things, even if they claim to! Right?"

"All the answers can be found within yourself, believe it or not. Sometimes the subconscious mind will reveal what's hidden though dream symbols. Do you have any repeating dreams that you can recall."

"Well, there is one ridiculous dream where I'm looking for my jewels, but I can't find them. Then, I'm in a forest, and I lose the path and don't know which way to go. Another one where I have to go to the bathroom, my pants are down while people are staring at me. Embarrassing, I know"

"Wow, where do we start with that one? What do you think the jewels symbolize?

"I don't know. I guess something valuable, something im portant to me?"

"And the path and the forest?"

"I guess, following the way I'm supposed to go, being on my true path."

"Very good. And the need to go to the bathroom."

"I don't know, but when I think about it, even now, I feel like shaking, I'm so embarrassed."

"Let's work with that one. Close your eyes and see yourself having to go to the bathroom. Your pants are down and people are looking at you. Now, go back in time and see if you can hit on any memories that trigger a similar feeling."

"Hmm...ok...I'm remembering being about twenty years old and my boyfriend is looking at me with lust in his eyes and I feel embarrassed."

"Good. Now go back even farther and see what is at the root of this feeling."

"Oh my God! I had completely forgotten that experience

135

until just now. That was a biggie."

"Can you talk about it?"

"It wasn't abuse or anything. I was about three or four years old and I was in a supermarket with my father. It was a long line and finally we were second in line, and I pulled on my daddy's pant leg and told him I have to pee. He said, 'Wait, we're next in line and then we can go.' I pulled again and repeated my request, with a bit more intensity. Next thing I know, pee was falling on the floor next to the checkout counter. He scooped me up and ran to the bathroom, yelling in a hushed voice through clenched teeth, saying: *You have totally embarrassed me. That was a very bad girl!* And something in me just shut down. I felt like a dog with its tail between its legs."

"That was excellent recall, Jennifer. This is big. Can you feel how that shame has colored other areas of your life?"

"I guess I have a feeling of shame over normal bodily functions—my sexual organs in particular."

"Well, I can tell you one thing for sure. You're not a bad girl!"

With that, tears started streaming out of the corners of Jennifer's eyes and down her cheeks. "Why am I crying?" she wondered, "That's silly."

"Feelings aren't silly, Jennifer. They are your jewels! Now, I want you, the adult you, the wise and compassionate mother you, to go to that little girl and tell her what is true about her on that day in the supermarket."

"You mean, pretend I'm there and she can hear me?"

"Just say to her what is in your heart. Take her from your father and hold her in your arms, stroke her hair, wipe the tears off her cheeks, and tell her the truth."

"I'm here for you, darling. You are not a bad girl. You told him you had to go and it is normal for full bladders to pee when they're very full. You did nothing wrong. You are forgiven. It's okay to forgive yourself."

"Now ask her to forgive her father."

"Daddy doesn't really think you're bad. He was just ashamed at himself for not listening to you when there was still time. He was embarrassed about not looking like a perfect dad in front of strangers. You are still, and always will be, his special little girl."

"See him hug you now and accept you for the wonderful child you really are."

With that, Jennifer put her face in her hands and sobbed more loudly than she would have liked, but these were feelings that did not want to be suppressed.

Sophia concluded with these words: "Jennifer, you have done a lot of good work. I am so proud of you! We can work on other issues during another visit. But you can practice this inner-child work whenever you find difficult emotions coming up."

"But my father is dead. How can I work out my issues with him?"

"Your father is doing fine—it's the father aspect of yourself that you've internalized which needs some work. We can do more of that later. I want you to also think of your father not as an all-knowing powerful being, but a flawed human, with positives and negatives, like we all have. He may have had unresolved issues from his own childhood that he never worked on."

"I remember that my grandparents, his parents, were pretty critical of him and his decisions, and that would make him really angry."

"Good, that will help you forgive him that much easier. But that path you are finding in the forest, it is the path to your Real Self. It is the message from your son that you must find out who you really are. I think you are now on that path."

CHAPTER 19

A Diet Change for Mom

Jennifer stayed in bed a few moments longer, allowing herself to just free associate, and soon, it bubbled up in her mind that she needs to improve her diet. She went online and looked up some keywords like: nutritionist, pregnancy, holistic, and found someone that was only a few miles away. She called and was able to get in the same day.

"Hi, I'm Jennifer."

"I'm Rochelle. I'm looking forward to helping you with your diet. I've already read your intake form."

"I'm a little scared, I have to admit. I have always just eaten the foods I like and enjoy. I don't want to feel like I'm eating cardboard."

"Don't worry, healthy foods are simple to prepare; they're more delicious and easier to find than ever. I know you are pregnant already, so we don't want to change too much too fast, as your body might cleanse or discharge toxins too quickly and we don't want to stress the baby."

"I like the idea of slow change anyway."

"So, I notice that a lot of your food choices are based on wheat, dairy, corn, sugar, and red meat. That is what our society has been using as staples for many decades, and while some people can handle them in moderation, many others don't do well with them at all. I think you could scale these back a bit."

"That makes me nervous. I'm used to ordering in pepperoni pizza, going out for a cheeseburger, and having nachos."

"How about this? We will focus on all the good foods that you'll be increasing in your diet and these other foods can then move to the periphery."

"Okay. I like that approach."

"Research is proving that a plant-based diet is often the most healthy. So, let's start with adding fresh foods like vegetables, fruits, beans, nuts and seeds. What vegetables do you eat now?"

"Salad, corn, tomato, potatoes..."

"What does a salad look like for you?"

"Oh, I guess I usually use iceberg lettuce, tomatoes, cucumbers and thousand-island dressing."

"That's a good start, now let's try to change things up a bit. Try a deeper green lettuce, like Romaine. It will contain more vitamins and minerals. Try to buy organic whenever you possibly you can. We don't want the little one absorbing too many pesticides or herbicides, they're very toxic. Try adding different colors—try 'tasting the rainbow' with radishes, carrots, kale, red cabbage, and purple cauliflower. I'll give you a list of vegetables to try, and you can add a few every week. All these would be great: rutabaga, turnips, snap peas, watercress, parsley, winter squash, and sweet potatoes."

"I love sweet potatoes, but I thought they were only for Thanksgiving!"

"Well, now you can give thanks every day! So, besides raw and cooked vegetables, add some vegetarian proteins, like beans. Besides the typical kidney and pinto beans, try some new ones like: adzuki beans, lentils, chickpeas and hummus."

"I like hummus! I tried it at a Greek restaurant."

"Great! Also, add some nuts every day, like almonds, walnuts, pecans and cashews, as well as seeds like pumpkin, sesame, and sunflower. For added Omega 3s, add some hemp seeds, ground flax seeds and chia seeds. I'm also going to suggest that you take some fish oil with DHA for the baby's developing brain. One big improvement will be to replace those store-bought dressings with a simple home-made oil and vinegar dressing. Use a good-quality olive oil with balsamic or apple-cider vinegar, organic herbs on salads, and use coconut or avocado oils for higher-heat cooking.

"I'd like you to start reading labels more closely. If you see canola oil, often disguised as vegetable oil, avoid it—that alone will help you quite a bit. For milk, switch it up a bit, there are so many out there like flax milk, hemp milk, coconut milk, almond milk, and others. Just make sure get the unsweetened kind, you can always add a few drops liquid stevia to make it sweeter. If you want some dairy, try some fermented, organic dairy, like yogurt or kefir. It's more digestible than non-fermented dairy products. Again, be sure to get the unsweetened ones, then you can add organic fruit or sugar-free granola."

"Aren't I going to be hungry all the time? I already am as the baby gets bigger."

"It is more so the oils and the proteins that will fill you up. I think it will be for the best if you can cut out pork and cured meats like hot dogs. If you really want occasional red meat, grass-fed, free-range beef would be better, even fresh game meats. More often, though, have poultry or wild-caught fish, but do avoid canned tuna while pregnant, because of its high mercury content. Snacking on nuts between meals will help to fill you up."

"What about desserts? I'm kind of used to them after meals."

"Well, I strongly recommend that my clients stay off of all corn-syrup and white-sugar products. When your blood sugar gets balanced over time, your cravings will decrease. The best is just to enjoy the naturally sweet taste of fruit. If you really need sugar, then stay with the natural sweeteners, like rice syrup, real maple syrup, or honey. There is also stevia, which is derived from a Bolivian herb. It has no calories but even just 5 drops or half a teaspoon of the powder in a bowl of oatmeal will make it taste sweet."

"I haven't had oatmeal in years."

"The steel-cut organic oats should be fine for you and your baby. There are several cooked grains that don't include wheat or corn. Try quinoa, brown rice, millet, barley and rye. Chew them well, eat them in moderation and you should be fine. I don't think you are gluten sensitive like many others, but just make wheat more occasional.

"But I love my morning bagels!"

"Just eat the holes! No, seriously, there are many new bread varieties out there without wheat. We don't want to change everything at once for you, but find gluten-free breads, like millet bread, or older forms of wheat that are not as hybridized, like spelt.

"Wow, I'm going to be busy, but I hope I don't give birth to a rabbit!"

"*Ha ha!* No chance of that! So that's enough to start with. Ease into these new foods. Soon, they will start tasting great. Over time, you will start feeling more energy and mental clarity, even your skin will start to look better. You'll be surprised, Jennifer. You will soon be craving these new, healthier foods and you might even notice that the pepperoni pizza starts tasting a bit too salty as well as not feeling very good in your stomach. When you do use salt, get sea salt or Himalayan salt, and just use a few pinches a day, mostly in cooking. This diet is a big change for you, but don't force it on your older children. Just have them taste it and set the example. Soon, they'll be curious and will open up to new ideas."

"I'll admit, I'm a bit overwhelmed, but I have my iPad in my kitchen. I'll look up recipes, and like you said, I'll just slowly add new things."

"Soon, you will have your new favorite kinds of food and you won't even miss the old ways. I have a feeling it won't be long before it will hard to find anything with wheat or white sugar in your kitchen anymore."

"Rochelle, thank you so much for your time and expertise. I have heard of some of these things and ignored them, but now I guess it actually does apply to me too. I realize I'm eating for two now, so I'm ready!"

"You go, girl! Please email me with any questions. We can meet again in a few months and do a follow-up."

"I look forward to that! I'm sure I'll have many questions."

CHAPTER 20

Consulting a Priest

Stuart was excited to hear of the progress Jennifer had made in her visit with the counselor. "Maybe you won't be so pissed off at me and the boys, now that your inner child has healed her inner bladder."

"Very funny."

"But seriously, even though we only go to church twice a year, I thought that it would be good for you to have a talk with our priest about your spiritual self. That seems like it would be a key part be part of finding out who you really are."

"I guess if anybody would know, it would be a priest. I'm willing to talk to him."

It turned out that Father Callahan was available to talk that evening.

After introducing themselves and settling into the large brown leather chairs, Jennifer laid her problem before the priest.

"You see, Father, I have been depressed ever since having a dream that my future son said that I had to find out who I really am in order to properly parent him. Can you help me?"

The priest nodded thoughtfully and said, "Mmm, I see. Amidst all the weddings, confirmations, baptisms and funerals, that is something I am not asked very often. I would say that from the perspective of the Church, you are a soul created by God."

"When was I created, millions of years ago, or recently?"

"Well, I haven't really thought about it, but I suppose you were created at the moment of conception. According to Church doctrine you are born a sinner, as we all are, for Adam and Eve sinned and we have all inherited that original sin. But, if you accept Jesus as your lord and savior and have faith in him, you will be saved and have eternal life. We are conceived in sin and only Jesus was without sin, being born of a virgin."

"I think I'm a pretty good soul and I don't really know about Adam, but I don't feel ashamed just from being born."

"I can only tell you the teachings of the Church on these matters."

Stuart then cleared his throat and said, "With all due respect, Father, I lack confidence in your authority in answering our questions. Did you know the word sin is an old archery term for missing the mark? We have to aim better, but just because we are not yet perfect doesn't make us, at our core, sinners."

The priest wasn't expecting a debate. He straightened up his back and stated, "I believe we must accept our fallen nature before we can be saved by the divine providence of God through his only begotten son Jesus the Christ."

"Do you really believe that story we have been told every Christmas that Jesus' parents never conceived their son in the normal way that everybody else has been for thousands of years?"

"The Bible does say that Jesus was born of a virgin."

"I have read that the word 'maiden' was more appropriate and that it is a mistranslation to indicate she was a virgin. I think it takes away the importance of the role of the father and makes Jesus so different from us that we can hardly strive to be like him."

Jennifer offered an idea, "Maybe the immaculate conception is a state of mind, of her only perceiving the perfection of her son in her mind, having no false conceptions of what he would be."

"The Church has been dispensing the truth of the Gospel as written in the Bible since Peter and we don't have to reason or think or assume to know the truth. A lot of it is a mystery. Still

144

though, the religious scholars do agree that Jesus was born from a virgin, Mary."

Stuart, starting to get a little upset by the dogma, said, "Father, have you ever had your own spiritual experiences, or do you just repeat to your flock what you have been told by the religious scholars?"

"Well I...um... I did feel a tangible sense of peace when I decided to become a priest and also when I am saying the Mass."

"That's it? After all these years, that is all you have of direct experience with the Spirit? No wonder priests can become lost... it makes me wonder why some people go into the profession in the first place, as evidenced by the number of pedophiles being exposed in the Church's ranks."

"Stuart, how can you say that?" Jennifer gasped.

"I'm sorry. That was a low blow."

Father Callahan looked ashen and shaken, wiping a tear from his eye he responded, "No, you are right. You hit a nerve there, for I have recently found out that my own mentor has been accused by seven different altar boys, now grown men, of pedophilia. The settlements will cost the Church many millions."

"I am so sorry, Father," breathed Jennifer.

"It's all right. Perhaps you are onto something. We priests are expected to counsel depressed pregnant women, people considering divorce, parents of young children, and matters regarding marriage and sexuality, and yet unlike rabbis and Protestant ministers, we are not allowed to marry, raise children, or have physical relations."

Jennifer got up and put on her jacket, as did Stuart and put her hand on the priest's shoulder and said, "Thank you for your time, father."

He looked up and said, "Thank you both for coming for

guidance and for having the courage to challenge my pat answers. I must look deeper into these matters. Please, come to my sermon this Sunday. I have a feeling it will be a wee bit out of the ordinary."

"Ok," Stuart said, "We will be there."

As they left, he called out, "And bring the kids!"

CHAPTER 21

An Unforgettable Sermon

onvincing Roger and Aiden to get up early on a Sunday morning to go to church was no easy matter. They had planned on playing Call Of Duty with their friends, but after being told they would go out for a big brunch afterwards, they consented—just this once.

The boys were glad that they were playing some Jesus-themed rock music before what they expected to be a boring sermon, although their parents sincerely doubted that Jesus and the saints were dancing to that beat. It seemed the Church was resorting to these tactics to get the younger people coming in, and at least the words are all positive.

People murmured a bit and looked around at each other questioningly as they saw a much calmer yet bleary-eyed Father Callahan coming to the podium, wearing a frock that was violet and not his usual brown. He cleared his throat, paused as he looked over his congregation, and with a comforting smile, began:

"You know me as Father Callahan, but please, for today you can know me by my first name, which is Frank—and let me be frank with you." When the ripple of laughter subsided, he continued, "Excuse me if I seem a bit tired, I have slept less than usual. I have been in deep prayer and inner turmoil. I have been working on this sermon for the last five days. A child of God came to me last week and needed some help in discovering her true identity. I realized that without my own knowledge of my true self, how could I increase her understanding? I stand before you a humbled man. When I was a toddler, I came to the Church full of wonder. I loved to watch the sun's rays playing thought the stained-glass windows. I loved the candles and the fancy clothes the priests wore with their majestic golden staffs. I relished hearing the parables of Jesus, and the stories of the saints and prophets... But then a priest took me into a confessional to sit on his lap, and all I can say is that it should have been him who confessed. I wanted him to touch my soul, but instead he touched my body. I have never recovered since that time—a part of me has felt bad and unclean. When I took my vows, especially of celibacy, I thought I could cut myself off from both pain and pleasure. I can say honestly that I have never hurt a child in that way, nor would I ever. It is said in the Bible that there is a sin against the Holy Spirit that is not forgiven. It does not spell out what that sin is, but if I were to offer a guess, I would say it is the abuse of a child, for that pain, guilt and shame goes deep into the soul of one who is young and innocent, and can perpetuate itself, poisoning future generations. I was painfully reminded the other day by a scientist that I have not had much in terms of my own spiritual experiences.

"I have been mouthing the same words and platitudes that have been mouthed by priests and religious scholars for centuries, but how do I know in my soul that they are all true?"

The audience gasped when Father Callahan said this.

"*The Bible says so* is what I have been told and what I have told others. Is that a good enough answer? Well, I can tell you that this past week I did indeed have a spiritual experience. The Holy Spirit, and I believe Jesus himself, inspired me to log on to the Internet. Keywords flowed into my mind, ideas and opinions that before then I would have considered heresy started to come into my awareness more and more. I could see that there was much truth that I had never even considered possible before.

"Can you believe we have almost no information about the life of Jesus, the most famous man in the world? There is a brief comment about his birth, a mention of fleeing to Egypt, then a snippet about impressing and confounding the doctors in the temple at age thirteen. Suddenly, he is thirty being baptized at the River Jordan and for three brief years he taught and performed his miracles, then he was crucified. There is a mention of his resurrection and his appearing to the disciples for 40 days, and then a description of his ascension from Bethany's hill. That's it? The church is silent on what he was doing between the ages of thirteen and thirty, which is more than half his life.

"Did he amaze the rabbis at age thirteen, only to sink into obscurity and work as a carpenter for most of his young life? I thought that if these missing years were known about, the Church would have told us. Well, I looked up the *Lost Years of Jesus* on the Internet, and found more that I could imagine. It seems that as a teenager and young man, Jesus traveled extensively throughout the Far East. There are well-documented legends of a *Saint Issa*, as they called him, seeking out and studying with the learned and enlightened masters and priests of his day. At least four separate individuals at the turn of the century told of being shown scriptures by Tibetan lamas proving that Jesus visited among them. There are recorded sermons where he preached on the honor of women and many other teachings not found in the traditional scriptures of today.

"God knows we could have used that teaching on the blessedness of women for these 2000 years. He preached to the lowest castes in India, called the untouchables, that God was their Father and loved them, too, for which the Brahmins tried to kill him, but he was let out of the city walls in a basket, just as he escaped from those who were so angered and would have killed him during his ministry in Galilee. Maybe he wasn't born a perfect Son of God after all, but had to search, struggle and learn, and come into the full mastery he demonstrated once his public ministry began with the wedding at Cana. Maybe this is a teaching our own teens need as they search out their own unique path and service.

"I have been taught that the Bible is the inspired word of God. But, it was written down, copied and edited many times by the scribes. The early church fathers may have had their own agendas, perhaps of keeping the people under their control, perhaps keeping them in the dark about their own innate divinity, which we can still plainly see in snippets of Jesus' teachings, such as in John 10:34, 'Is it not written in your Law, I said, You are gods?'

"Another example of possible tampering is in Matthew 14:14, where it is written: 'Jesus, moved with compassion, said, *Be healed,*' but when an older and more original form of the Bible was discovered, it said, 'Jesus, *enangered, said, Be healed!*' Some conjecture that a priest or copyist decided that Jesus was too nice and too perfect to ever be angry, so this part was changed to *moved with compassion.* It is usually told to us that the only time Jesus showed anger was when he overturned the moneychangers' and vendors' tables in the Hebrew temple early on in his ministry. He often impatiently exposed the hypocrisy of the high priests, and even is said to have reacted to the incessant request by people to be healed by him by answering: *Heal yourselves!*

"What else could have been edited out of our Scriptures? In my research over the last few days, I read about an early Church Father named Origen of Alexandria who was one of the main teachers of Christianity in his day. He lived around the year A.D. 200 and said of the Bible that it contains three levels of meaning, which correspond to the threefold Pauline (and Platonic) division of a person into body, soul, and spirit.

"The bodily level of Scripture, the bare letter of the law, is normally helpful as it stands to meet the needs of the more simple people. The soul or psychic level is for making progress in perfection for those embarking on a spiritual path. The spiritual interpretation deals with what for the less initiated remain as *unspeakable mysteries*, but remain for all those willing to walk the path of deeper initiations, 'partakers of all the doctrines of the Spirit's counsel.' So, Origen accepted that the simple-minded might benefit from the literal interpretation of the Bible, but there are deeper levels of meaning for deeper-thinking souls.

"As I dug deeper into my research, I began to uncover, even in the Bible of today, has references to reincarnation. Origen noted that in the *Book of Malachi*, it tells the story of two babies in their mother's womb, Jacob and Esau, and that God loved one and hated the other. Origen reasoned that if God is all-just and all-merciful, how could he randomly love one innocent child and not the other?

He concluded that the immortal soul of one child had lived in harmony with God's Laws of Love in previous lifetimes, while the other had violated those laws for many lifetimes.

"So, as it turned out, the literalists and orthodox priests ended up taking over the Church. It also became a highly politicized means of controlling the people once this new religion was taken over by Rome. Origen was soon labeled as a heretic and his teachings were declared anathema, denounced by the Pope. People were excommunicated from the Church for studying his writings.

"Do you know that more than half the world's population believes in reincarnation? I had never given it much thought until this week. I thought that if it were true, it would be spelled out in the Bible.

"So I wondered, myself, whether there were any references still in the Bible hinting at reincarnation and I did find some! In Matthew, Chapter 9, it tells about Jesus encountering a man who was blind from birth. His disciples asked him, 'Rabbi, who sinned—this man or his parents, that he was born blind?' Jesus goes on to say that, in private, he taught the disciples all things, but he taught the multitudes only in parables. Obviously, the disciples asked Jesus if the sin belonged to a newborn baby because they understood about reincarnation. The sin would have come from the karma of a sin carried over from a past life. In this case, though, Jesus answered that this was neither the sin of this soul, nor the sin of his parents—it was so that the work of God might be displayed in his life by Jesus' healing of his blindness.

"Then there is the part where the disciples are wondering about the prophecy in Malachi where Elijah would go before the Messiah. So, Jesus spoke of John the Baptist and said, 'And if you are willing to accept it, he is the Elijah who was to come again.' Interesting enough, even though the church likes to accept the literal interpretation of most scripture, here they would only say that it means he came *in the spirit and power of Elijah*.

"Now, we priests generally don't like it when our flock disagrees with the standard beliefs, but it used to be worse—a lot worse. In the 13th century, the Church murdered thousands of people, including women and children, because they considered themselves Christians but with differing beliefs. If you look it up, they were called the Cathars or Albigensians of France. They believed in reincarnation and refused to eat meat. They were strict about the biblical injunctions of not telling lies, not killing, and not swearing oaths. They considered men and women as equals and did not object to contraception. But perhaps their most fatal belief was that they refused to pay tithes to the Catholic Church. I had no idea about my own church's history and am now ashamed.

"How did this so-called orthodoxy, which means, literally, *having the right opinion,* arise? It took about 400 years for what we consider the books of the Bible to attain their present form. Before then, the Catholic Church was just one of dozens of faiths that had arisen from Jesus' original teachings. Catholicism was accepted as the state religion of the Roman Empire after the Emperor Constantine made it the official religion. After that, possession of *heretical literature* was punishable by death.

"Up until the last century, the only knowledge we had of Origen of Alexandria, or the Gnostics, and other early Christian beliefs was from the attacks upon them by the early church fathers. I learned that in 1945, a treasure trove of ancient Gnostic scriptures was found in Nag Hammadi, Egypt, parchments found in jars, written in the Coptic language. You can see why the Church attempted to wipe out all memory of them, as they showed a great respect for personal, spiritual experience, as opposed to orthodox dogma.

"In the Gnostic Gospel of Philip, it says, 'You saw the spirit; you became spirit. You saw Christ; you became Christ. You saw the Father; you shall become the Father.' In the Gospel of Thomas found at Nag Hammadi, Jesus says, 'I am not your master. Because you have drunk, you have become drunk from the bubbling stream that I have measured out. He who will drink from my mouth will become as I am. I myself shall become he, and the things that are hidden shall be revealed to him.'

"Gnosticism derives from the word, gnosis, which is a kind of built-in spiritual knowing of one's own true essence—of one's own divine origin as a spark originating in its Divine Source, which would make each of us a literal soul mate or 'twin' of Jesus.

"So, why am I telling you this? Why am I sacrificing my own profession to present to you a revelation I only just now received and don't fully understand yet? It is because a soul came to me and asked who she really was. I now believe she does have a divine spark within her heart, which is in constant contact with our Creator. So do I, and so do you. Paul never met Jesus and yet received all his teachings directly from Jesus in the ascended state. Why shouldn't this woman, or any of us, do the same?

"I suppose this will be my last sermon from this beloved altar. I do thank you for letting me serve you all of these years. But in all honesty, without my own meditation and my own inner experience, I doubt that I can lead you to where you need to go."

Nobody knows who started it. Some say it was a young person, some say it was an angel—Jennifer even felt that it arose from her unborn baby—but slowly and softly at first, people started chanting, "Stay, Father Frank... Stay, Father Frank!" Soon they were clapping as well. Of course, once the bishop heard about it, he never let Father Callahan preach another sermon. But he did start an online blog as well as a study and meditation group on the deeper teachings of esoteric Christianity. Narayan's parents were among them.

There is talk about starting a new church based upon his revelations, but for now, they are satisfied with their progress as an informal spiritual community. He says in his mission statement that, "To give the living path of Truth to the youth," is a main part of his work now. Even Aiden and Roger have joined his youth group—they are exercising more, playing less video games, and learning to look within themselves to always let their conscience be their guide. "J.C. is Jiminy Cricket or Jesus Christ, the same as your inner voice," is what Father Frank tells them.

B altar patted his disciple on the back. "Narayan, I must admit I didn't think that the dream you gave your mother that night would have such a far-reaching impact."

"Imagine, Jesus himself interceded and guided Father Callahan's mind in his online searching to find out so many mysteries of the Christ."

"I have looked down his lifestream and found that he had a few things in his favor. He was a master of invocation on Atlantis, thus he still has a great mastery of the Word, spoken and written. He was actually one of the Cathars that were killed in that mountaintop siege during the Albigensian Crusade waged by the Pope. He was also a teacher of Buddhism in Ancient China. His mastery of meditation will again return, and he will assist you in going within for guidance."

"Incredible! Also, my two older brothers have really been transforming. I'm looking forward to being their little brother now. My parents just didn't know how to compete with all the electronics, violence and peer influences in their lives."

CHAPTER 22

Meditation

N arayan mused, "There are so many conflicting vibrations down there, with TV, Wi-Fi, satellites, cell phones, microwaves, discordant music. How will I be attuned to my own frequencies and those from higher levels?"

Renatia explained more deeply. "Narayan, you now understand the scientific laws of frequency, as well as how we create here in the realms of spirit. All is vibration. The Lord created all in his mind, but in order to make it manifest, he sent forth The Word. Sound vibrations penetrate the various dimensions and the energy coalesces into patterns. The stronger the mental visualization, the more intense the desire, and the clearer the sound, the more successful the precipitation will be. This is true alchemy. Here, where we dwell in the etheric, all precipitations manifest immediately, but in the realm of time and space, there is a lag between the perception of what is to be created and its manifestation."

Baltar continued, "Those who have made the effort to study, and those who have become successful in life, have universally understood that it is the one-pointedness, determination, and desire for the goal that has enabled its achievement."

Narayan laughed, "And when we finally get what we want, we often find out that it wasn't what we really needed after all!"

"That is why Jesus said: *Seek ye first the Kingdom of God and his righteousness and all these things will be added unto you.* You see, the Kingdom of God is the Consciousness of God. In this state, you are a co-creator with the universal Creator, and when your will is aligned with God's will, you will not only get what you want, what you want will also be what you need."

Narayan felt that someone was reaching out to him on the inner. He closed his eyes and took some deep breaths. He calmed his mind and found himself seated on a *zafu*, a meditation cushion, across from Sephira in a beautiful meditation chamber.

"I knew I could do it—I just knew I could transport you here!" Sephira exclaimed.

"This is amazing! What is this place?"

"I took advantage of the fact that you were napping in the womb. I thought I might connect with you now. This is where I have been taking meditation classes. I wanted to invite you here to join me. Meditating with others creates more of a forcefield and all can go deeper."

"I have been meaning to look into it. I know that as the stress levels go up and up on planet Earth, we are going to need all the tools we can use to stay cool, calm and collected."

"I have learned so many ways of meditating. You just have to keep trying until you find whatever works best for you. The main thing is to stop the *monkey mind* from wandering, to either silence it or to focus on just one point in the present moment, such as on a mandala."

"I have heard that just focusing on the breath going in and out, like waves on the shore, can be one way to calm the mind."

"Yes, a slow and steady breath allows the mind to settle in the moment and calms the nerves. At first, I focused on a candle flame and after many attempts, there was no separation between subject and object—the flame disappeared and yet I was the flame."

"I have heard that chanting sacred sounds can be a powerful entryway into meditation."

"Yes, I chanted the sacred *OM* of creation until I could actually hear the inner sound vibration that permeates the Cosmos. Of course, this is easier in these higher realms than it is on Earth because we are closer to the source. Even on Earth, in deep meditation, one can enter these realms and absorb not only all the wisdom of these higher levels, but the light of even higher levels than here."

"That must be hard to experience when in a physical body."

"On Earth, the attention is usually always directed outwards to the senses. One must turn those searchlights inwards to cut off the sensory input and go deep within the soul in silence. Then, you will see inner lights and wonders, eventually feeling the bliss of the Spirit and the wonderful *peace of God, which passeth all understanding.*"

"I'd love to get started. What do you want to meditate on right now?"

"Let's focus on the flame in the center of the heart chakra, where our spiritual identity is anchored."

"Narayan was surprised by how difficult it was to keep his mind attentive to just one thing—it wandered from thought to thought: *Sephira is so beautiful. I wonder what being a baby on Earth will be like. Maybe I should take some meditation lessons from Gomasio. Okay, back to the heart flame.*

Sephira whispered gently, "Even the Buddha when in embodiment struggled to reach the highest states. He just stayed under that Bodhi Tree and vowed not to get up from his meditation until he reached enlightenment. Then he downloaded the teachings—*The Four Noble Truths and the Noble Eightfold Path*—that are still guiding millions of Buddhists after 2500 years."

Narayan steeled his mind. He was determined to experience that heart flame directly, not just thinking about it or imagining it. After several attempts, he finally let go and just was. Then there was a *whoosh*—a bright light filled his mind and he saw a flame, pulsing steadily; it filled him with bliss. He tried to enter into the flame, but all of a sudden, got scared of losing himself and fell back into normal waking consciousness.

"I did that the first few attempts, too," said Sephira knowingly. "I found it helpful to chant the Tibetan mantra, *Om mani padme hum,* to myself quietly. This sacred mantra has many meanings and for right now, a good one is: *Hail to the jewel in the center of the lotus,* which is the heart chakra."

Narayan responded, "I'm going to work on this every day. I am determined to imprint this practice into my soul so that when I'm on Earth, I can find out about this at a young age, so as to never lose my center to outer circumstances or discord."

Sephira waxed with enthusiasm, "The meditation teachers here have often been yogis and mystics who lived in caves in the Himalayas. Now they are overshadowing researchers who are proving again and again how mindfulness and meditation is more powerful for healing in general, and depression in particular, than any medicine."

"I have a great bumper sticker: *Don't medicate—meditate!* But what do you mean by mindfulness, as opposed to meditation?"

"Instead of just being seated with straight spine and closed eyes, as a regular, everyday practice, you can just be mindful of being in the present moment. On Earth, the illusion of time is much stronger than it is here. People often live in the past, revolving old memories, or worrying about a future that may or may not come to pass. But the present moment is the only place that's real. We are constantly born anew and free in the NOW! Fear, anger and sadness all have to do with past and future. When you wash the dishes, don't wish for it to be over so you can do something else. Feel the water; listen to its sounds. Be aware of your sponge scrubbing; make it a meditation. When walking in nature, see the miracles of the sky, the trees and the animals. Hear the rustling wind and the babbling brook. Smell the forest. The bliss of being in the moment is immense and can be more satisfying and permanent than any drug induced experience. It is being *high on life itself* that is available in the suchness of each moment."

CHAPTER 23

An Inner-Sight Visit to a Hospital

N
arayan had an idea, "Why don't we both visualize a giant flame between us, and just focus on that with one-pointed attention."

They sat still and slowly started feeling a burning in their hearts. The temperature felt like it was heating up. Then a giant white flame about seven feet high precipitated between them, and to their surprise, a tall white-fire angel stepped forth into their midst and declared:

"I am Ramiel, one of the seraphim of the sacred fire of God's purity and light! We are angels closest to the source of creation. I have come in answer to the meditation of your hearts. I come with a lesson for you in the art of spiritual self-defense and to expose the forces that have arrayed themselves in opposition to the Light!"

After a long pause of amazement, Sephira addressed the seraph: "Ramiel, we are grateful for your presence. Please, show us what you can about how the beings of shadow keep the people of Earth in darkness and defeat."

"I give you both a helmet of white light to protect your mind and I ask you to don this white-fire armor of protection. Go into meditation again and I will transport us to a place on earth where the dark ones operate. Take this shield of light in your left hand and this fiery sword in your right. The more you visualize their action, the more powerful they will become."

As they went deep within, they could sense a rushing sound and the feeling of rapid movement. As this slowed down, they felt an increased sense of density and oppression. They opened their eyes and found themselves on the eighth floor of a hospital in Chicago, in the psych ward. First, Ramiel touched his two protégés on the forehead and whispered, "This is what the nurses and doctors see." People mulled about in hospital gowns, some muttering under their breath with glazed eyes—others crammed in the smoking room, watching the TV mounted on the wall above them. One was yelling at a doctor, calling him a Nazi who was experimenting on him.

"Now see what this scene is like when viewed from the astral sight" and he touched their third eyes again.

"Whoa" is what they both breathed in unison. The smokers all had what looked like a giant worm wrapped around their bodies and sank its teeth into their foreheads. When they inhaled it relaxed its pressure, giving them a sense of temporary peace and respite.

Narayan whispered, "What are those things?"

"Tobacco entities. Every addiction has its own variation of entities. They drive the addict to repeat their habit and only give them a brief release when they fulfill their desire."

Sephira looked around the floor and noticed grey shadows surrounding the people shuffling around the hall. "What are those?"

Ramiel replied, "Those are discarnate entities, often called ghosts. They are the astral shells or emotional bodies of those who have passed on. They are no longer attached to the incarnate soul and thus have no source of energy of their own, so they latch onto the energy fields of those who have a weakened or ruptured aura and try to have their needs met vicariously through one in embodiment. They may look like the person who has died, but the soul is no longer present."

Ramiel pointed to the man who had been yelling at the doctor. In the center of the grey energy field was a focus of intense, fiery crimson. "That is a demon that has latched onto the ghost or discarnate—much more dangerous. This is common among those with severe psychosis."

"What are those?" Sephira asked as she pointed to the grids of energy floating around in the atmosphere.

"Oh, those are thoughtforms. When people have repeating thoughts and ideas, they coalesce as forms on the mental plane that can overtake people and then they will start to have those same thoughts. Someone might be in a good mood and then sit on a bus seat and afterwards feel depressed, not realizing that they have picked up a floating thoughtform."

Narayan pointed to one, "Look! There is one with a cross in the middle. What if I just nudge it over to that guy shuffling over there?" With his intention, the cloud drifted and touched the guy in his head area. Suddenly he became more awake and started saying loudly, "I am Jesus... I have come to heal you all... I can walk on water."

The nurse said to one of the interns, "That's the first thing he has said all week, but he isn't very creative. That's the third time someone has made that claim this week."

The patient with the red demon attached to the ghost starting yelling again: "You are all Nazis. You are going to gas us in the showers."

Ramiel pointed his sword at the red figure, shot out a bolt of white lightning, removed it from his aura, and suspended it near the ceiling. Suddenly, the man became calm and looked around him, as if waking from a dream, saying, "Where am I, and what am I doing here?"

Narayan said, "Wow, we could empty this ward if we just started blasting all these entities!"

Suddenly, the astral beings started becoming agitated and could start seeing the unwelcome visitors. A swarm of grey, black and red beings started to surround the threesome. Out of the shadows came dark, giant spiders, scorpions and cobras.

"Shields up!" demanded Ramiel. "On three, blast the light out of your swords at these creatures—one, two, three!"

Light shot out from their extended swords like bolts of lightning. The entities that weren't obliterated were cut into pieces that only slowly came together again. Others hid in dark corners and under beds. Patients started filing out of the smoking room. They started speaking sensibly to each other. Two took up a game of ping pong. Others shot pool, while others commented on the politics they had seen on the news. The nurses looked around confused. It had never been like this before; everyone was so calm and rational.

Narayan exclaimed, "Wow, I think we better get out of here before we put this place out of business. Ramiel spoke to his charges, "This will bring only temporary relief to these patients, depending on their karmic patterns. Let's hope they gain some benefit from the reprieve. Time to move on."

They started descending through the floor until they got to fourth level, the Intensive Care Unit.

"Clear!" yelled the doctor as he held the paddles on both sides of the patient's chest. There was an electrical sound as his body convulsed and arched a few inches from the bed. The heartbeat was still flat-lined. "Again!" yelled the surgeon and he charged the paddles again, "Come on! Beat, you bastard!" Again, there was no response. Then, something quite amazing happened that no one but the invisible visitors could see.

The patient's soul was floating above the body and drifting higher and higher. The silvery cord that connected him to his body was fraying and losing its luminosity. Then, Narayan could see what looked like a lasso coming from below. It came from the hospital's chapel. The patient's wife and two children were on their knees praying. Eight miles away, members of their church were also praying and their energy surged into the hospital's chapel through the hearts of his kneeling family. This accumulated prayer energy was what formed the spiritual rope that was gently pulling the man's soul back into his body. *Beep, beep, beep* went the electrocardiogram (EKG) unit as the machine showed a heartbeat again.

The doctor looked up, amazed, and just whispered, "Thank God!"

After a few minutes, the man opened his eyes and his family rushed in and hugged him. All were crying.

"I saw it all," said the patient. "I was floating near the ceiling. I saw the doctor and his machine. I saw you all praying in the chapel. It looked like you were sending me beautiful lights. I heard all the prayers from church rising up to God to

intercede for me. I know I still have work to do here. I'm so glad I came back, and now, I know I won't be afraid when it's really my time to die."

The doctor had heard all this and took his patient's hand, "I thought we lost you there. I almost gave up, and now, here you are. I have heard reports of people being conscious while out of their bodies, but have never heard it firsthand."

"Well, doctor, I can tell you this: my heart has a father and thus, it's not a bastard!"

"Wow, I guess you could still hear me, even though I would have declared you dead at that moment!"

Sephira mentioned to Ramiel, "That doctor seems to be so dedicated to keeping his patients alive."

"It was not always like that. He is balancing his karma with each heart he repairs and saves. Here, look at this."

The seraph took his shield, turned it over and laid it on the floor. It lit up and projected a three-dimensional hologram in the space above. It showed an ancient, Aztec pyramid. A muscular priest with feathers in his hair took the stone knife and deftly cut open a live victim's chest, amid much screaming and torture. He reached in, cut out and removed the victim's heart and lifted it on high for all the crowd below to see. They all cheered. The blood ran down a stone trench and was gathered in a golden vessel as an offering to the gods.

Ramiel said, "Shocking, isn't it? But that is how it was in those days. That priest believed he protected the city and the crops with such an offering. In order to balance that karma, he has had many embodiments in which he died of heart diseases. Now as a surgeon, he is finishing off the remainder of his karma by working so hard to help heal as many hearts as he can. Often, the

patients he attracts are the exact people he sacrificed those many centuries ago."

Narayan asked, "Why did they believe that shedding the blood of sacrifices would help anything?

Ramiel replied, "The life-force is in the blood. The dark spirits on the astral plane need life energy, and blood is potent force. There are always dark spirits on the battlegrounds of the world, siphoning off the life-force. And it's not only the blood they're after—it's also the energy they siphon from people's anxiety, fear, rage and anger. All these things give energy to the beings of the shadow realm. Ah, we are being summoned. Close your eyes now. Go into a meditative state and relax your minds."

After another rushing sound, they found themselves seated in the meditation chamber that they had been in earlier. They stayed in deep meditation for some time. At first, Narayan couldn't stop thinking about the entities in the psych ward or the Aztec priest and his grisly sacrifice, but after a time, he kept coming back to his breathing. His mind settled and he felt a blissful peace returning to his soul.

CHAPTER 24

Forgiveness & Spiritual Practice

Baltar was seated in *Samadhi*—a deep, blissful state of oneness with the universal consciousness of Divine Love. Narayan and Sephira could feel the radiation from his aura charging them with a blessed light. Gradually, he opened his eyes while a beaming smile shone on his face. "As you both get closer to entering the physical plane, I want to make sure you really understand the use of the Law of Forgiveness."

Narayan responded, "I suppose it is deeper than just saying *I'm sorry* when you make a mistake."

"You really want to get to the level where you can transmute karma and negative attachments with forgiveness—both of yourself and of all others who you perceive to have wronged you."

Sephira spoke up: "I heard of a case, in a class on karma that I took, where a woman who was Jewish in her past life, died with such hatred for one of her Nazi captors, that they ended up being married in their next life—not a happy marriage."

Baltar thought for some time. "It is possible that if she died with the same thought that Jesus had on the cross toward his torturers—*Father, forgive them, for they know not what they do*—that they may not have formed that cord of hatred that continues to bind them together through non-forgiveness."

Narayan spoke, "I have heard that there are Tibetan monks who have been tortured by their Communist Chinese captors. These monks, instead of fighting back or blaming them, just meditate on total forgiveness and non-attachment."

"Yes, they have a very advanced teaching on the heart of

forgiveness. I recall one Tibetan monk who was thus tortured and forced to defile the holy books and Buddha statues. After he was freed, he was asked: 'What was the most painful and terrible part of being imprisoned and tortured?' and his reply was, 'I almost did not forgive my torturers.'"

Sephira asked, "Baltar, I have been working with my guides and it turns out that I am to be the subject of bullying in junior high school in my coming life. It seems that it is for a dual reason, I have bullied them in a past life, when I didn't know what I know now, and also, I am going to teach about how to overcome adversity and I need to have this experience as an example."

"Remember that no matter who you are with, you must learn to either love them, or if that is impossible, then at least to be neutral. It is when you want revenge, when you hold resentment and non-forgiveness, that you are creating binding ties and karmic knots with others that will draw you back together again in some future experience to resolve the energetic attachment."

Narayan asked, "What happens on the energetic levels when someone forgives?"

"Excellent question! But first I have a question for you— what is the highest frequency of color in the rainbow?"

Sephira and Narayan spoke up simultaneously, "Violet!"

"Correct! Now, I want you both to visualize and to start chanting: *I am forgiveness acting here... I am forgiveness acting here!* As you say this, you visualize being bathed in a joyous, loving, forgiveness flame of a deep violet color."

They started chanting and soon could actually see this violet flame dancing around them.

Baltar reminded Narayan, "Remember those seeds and samskaras I showed you in your astral body—those negative tendencies in your subconscious that could trip you up? Bathe them now in the violet consuming flame. This is a gift that is mostly known only by initiates in these inner retreats."

Narayan concentrated on a large seed near his solar plexus, which had to do with getting frustrated easily if the answers or solutions didn't come right away. He focused his attention there and it became like a violet-fire blowtorch. The seed gradually melted like butter on a frying pan—then with a whiff of gray smoke, it was gone.

"See? Now you will have more patience with yourself and trust that answers and solutions will come in due time. Let's take a break for now, but I want you both to daily do this forgiveness meditation, focusing on your prospective families, so that their burdens will be lighter. It will also help you to have an easier transition to the Earth plane."

Sephira asked, "How often should we do this kind of work?"

Baltar replied, "Everyone should have some form of *sadhana* or daily spiritual practice. While in embodiment, it is good to have a regular morning and evening practice. Some may do Yoga, Tai Chi, or Qigong, followed by meditation, prayer or chanting, and affirmations or decrees. The morning is often the most important part of the day, as you can more easily attune to your higher self. You can align yourself with your divine plan, which seems clear up here, but can easily be lost or forgotten in the density below. In these sessions, even down below, you should be able to open up to the angels and masters of light. It is even better if you can set aside a space for an altar, in a small room or corner of a room, used only for spiritual practice, as the energy will build up for you in that sacred space."

"What should we place on our altars?" Sephira queried.

"On a small table you could have a colored cloth with a crystal or glass chalice, symbolizing the soul as a perfect, clear vessel to hold spiritual light. You could also have some crystals and flowers, as well as pictures or statues of masters or angels. You can have photos of loved ones or images of people or situations you would like to pray for—even a globe so you can visualize blessing the whole world. As food is for people, so this is light for the angels. Especially when you pray at regular times, the angels go on their rounds and collect the light of prayers and bring them to where they need to go. The use of rituals will have a lot to do with the development of the Aquarian Age that is dawning. Take the power of one person in prayer and now multiply the effect by squaring the number of people who are praying together—in other words, if ten people are praying, the power of that prayer is ten-times-ten!"

Baltar continued, "When the love and devotion of the group builds and grows through prayer, song and teaching, there is built in the etheric planes what looks like a mighty cathedral of light. Rainbow rays of energy beam out from the spires of praise and bless the entire world. It is a most beautiful thing to behold and has literally kept the Earth whole and intact for thousands of years, but now, with the decline of group worship, we are seeing a fraying of the garment of protection around the world. Now, rather than going to churches and synagogues to pray, more people go to alcohol-filled noisy concerts where the dark forces can take all that dissipated energy and use it for their nefarious purposes. Some churches, to make money, are letting cellphone towers and antennas be put on their spires—a grave mistake."

Narayan asked, "Perhaps you can take us on a field trip to various services and concerts around the world so we can see these mass thoughtforms first hand."

Baltar answered, "A splendid idea. Although, I had a trip planned for you on a subject that you have asked me about a while ago."

"What was that?"

"You asked to be able to see for yourself what it was like to live on the lost continent of Atlantis."

"Oh, yes! I have often wondered if Atlantis was a real place or just imagined."

"Real, indeed! We can go to the Hall of Records and you can actually go back and see the revivified akashic records of what life was like back then. Off we go, then!"

CHAPTER 25

Records of Atlantis

As they walked through the giant, golden-peaked arches embossed with angels' wings, they read the inscription, "Those who do not learn from history are destined to repeat it." Baltar introduced Narayan and Sephira to an angelic librarian named Najdar.

"I will take you to an akashic viewing room. I understand you have a particular interest in Atlantis. I have done my own studies on the fall of that great continent and it has many parallels to what is occurring on Earth right now."

As they walked down a corridor lined with books and scrolls, Narayan asked, "What really is an akashic record?"

"Well, there is an everlasting exact recording of everything that happens in the universe. It is imprinted, like memory in the brain, but on the mind or memory of God. We here are able to take you to any point in time and space and allow you to see and experience history in action. Here are the chairs you will be using. Put these helmets on and lower the visor. I will place you in the capital of Atlantis."

Sephira asked, "Could you take us to a point past its heights, where it was beginning to fall? I feel that would be very instructive for us, as we are planning our descent into a culture that is also slipping toward decline."

"I know just the time, then. Settle in, go into meditation, and I will program the record. You will be able to question people or ask mental questions. The answers will telepathically be able to be understood and you will understand their language—although you can in no way change or affect history yourself. I will be available for any questions afterwards. Enjoy!"

They looked up and saw the sun shining with a golden light, illumining wonderful and intricately carved buildings. Many were pyramidal in shape. The streets were wide and formed circular patterns alternating with canals of water with majestic boats floating down them. There were long spindle-like flying ships noiselessly gliding in the air from place to place.

"You look as if you must be visitors," a young man who looked to be about twenty exclaimed, as he had been watching them look around in awe.

"We...we are visitors," Sephira stammered as she looked down and saw that they were dressed in what looked like togas.

"It's our first time in the city," explained Narayan.

"Well then, let me show you around Caiphul, the capital of Poseidon, the jewel of Atlantis."

"We would be most grateful. My name is Sephira and this is my friend, Narayan."

I am Waxul, a student here. I attend the university in the science track."

"Are there many other courses of study?" Narayan asked, interested.

"There are many courses, but two main schools, either science, or one may study at the Incalithlon in the religious track."

"What is your main focus?" asked Sephira.

"I am at a point where I have to declare my major. I am interested in the use of the giant crystals, the fire stones that power our civilization. I also have an interest in the engineering of life to produce new species to act as our servants."

"You mean this entire city, including the flying ships, are powered by crystals?" Narayan asked.

"Indeed, we have found that there is another dimension full of energy, we call it the night-side or Navaz Forces. It is an invisible energy source that can be channeled to our dimension though giant crystals that we have learned to work with."

"Whoa, what is *that* thing?" Narayan exclaimed, as he saw a two legged creature with talons and a beak pushing a stroller."

"We simply call them *things*. They were created through our experiments in genetic engineering. We have mixed human and animal cells together to produce workers to do those things we would rather not do. They are not very intelligent and they do not question our authority."

Sephira asked, "Can you tell me more about the religious track?"

"Well, of course, we all believe in *Incal*, the sun, who reigns supreme over all. But those at the Incalithlon study what is called the *Sun Behind the Sun*, and how the soul is related to the Infinite. I can take you to the Temple of the Sun, if you would care to see it."

"Indeed!" they both exclaimed.

They walked over a bridge above a canal, the sails of a boat just missing their feet. They approached a giant, golden pyramid and entered its golden gates. They were amazed to see what looked like giant stalactites hanging from the ceiling. There was an altar in the center with what looked like a giant, nine-foot flame blazing upon it with a book at its base, but the book was not consumed by the flame."

"Pretty amazing, isn't it? This is the Maxin Light. It is supposed to remind us of the underlying flame in our hearts. Many centuries ago, a great heavenly being gave us that Book of the Law and caused this flame to spring up from it. There is a prophecy that when the masses of people fail to live according to the Divine Law, the flame will go out and our nation will be destroyed. My grandparents believed in all of that, but we scientists are learning so much more than they ever knew. We are starting to doubt the old myths and fables more with every passing discovery."

Sephira looked at him amazed, "You have this living flame! How can you doubt?"

"It has been here for millennia. I guess we just take it for granted. It is considered a great honor, after one has died, to have one's body dropped into the flame, the body just disappears. We may see it happen if we wait here long enough."

Narayan asked, "Can you show us the main government building here in the capital?"

"Oh, sure. It is not far away. Follow me."

They walked outside the far side of the temple to see a large building with a giant snake carved around it, with its mouth wide open and stairs within. That was the main entrance.

"What kind of government do you have here?"

"Well, we are a democracy, of course."

"Everyone can vote?" Sephira asked.

"Only those who have graduated from either of the universities can vote. We couldn't have the uneducated vote, now, could we?"

"And who runs for office?" Narayan asked.

"Well, there are a group of spiritual adepts, called the Sons of the Solitude. They teach of something called the Law of the One. They have silently meditated for years in the forest and have realized the Self. They are unattached to all things, but they come out to be of service. We vote them into various offices, all the way to the *Great Rai* or King."

"Enlightened rulers! Can you imagine that? Now where

I come from..." mused Narayan, but Sephira stopped him.

"I must admit that some of us are beginning to question their authority. They won't allow us to use the new crystal lasers to conquer our enemies abroad. It is as if they do not revel in the glory of our fatherland!"

Waxul pulled out a small plate from a pocket in his cloak, and it glowed with an image of a man. "It is my teacher calling me. He wants me to go over my mistakes on my last exam."

"We can't thank you enough, Waxul!" Sephira said effusively.

"Good luck in your studies!" Narayan exclaimed.

"Enjoy your visit!" said Waxul, and he was off.

They both heard an inner, high-pitched noise, felt a little off-balance, and got a telepathic message to close their eyes. When they opened them again, they were back in the chairs with their helmets in the Hall of Records."

"Well, did you enjoy your immersive educational experience?" Najdar asked.

"That was incredible!" They both spouted.

"Najdar, I suppose that even a great civilization like that can't go on forever," Sephira mused.

"Pride, greed, overpopulation, exploitation of resources and allowing science and the intellect crowd out spirituality and intuition—we see it all the time. I have reviewed many civilizations and past golden ages."

"When were we visiting?" Narayan asked.

"That was about twelve thousand years ago. They did end up using their crystal lasers for war. They did terrible genetic experiments to create slaves and then powerful warriors. The Maxin Light eventually went out, and it was all downhill after that. There were many massive earthquakes and a truly giant flood."

"Was that the story of Noah?" Sephira wondered.

"Indeed. Most cultures have stories of a great flood that decimated most of their ancestors."

"Where was this capital city of Caiphul?" Narayan asked.

"It was where the Caribbean Islands are now. Those are the mountaintops of Atlantis.

"But I read that Plato said Atlantis was near the Strait of Gibraltar. Isn't that near Spain?"

"I am impressed that you are so well-read. There was, in fact, a series of disasters at that time. A few, like Noah, had warning. They survived and started new cultures, such as in ancient Egypt. It was an Egyptian priest who told Plato about the fall of a latter outpost of Atlantis, which fell only a few thousand years before the apex of ancient Greece."

"I suppose we should learn something from all of this?" Narayan wondered.

"I hear that you are both descending to be born in the United States of America. Well, that proud nation is nothing more than Atlantis come again, with many Atlantean souls.

Surprising them from behind was their beloved teacher. "And that is why I have sent you here," Baltar laughed as he placed his hands on both their shoulders, "so you could be part of the solution and steer people away from the same folly that destroyed such a high culture."

"I hear genetic engineering is going full-steam ahead," Narayan noted.

"It says in Genesis that the Lord God decreed that every seed should bear only after its own kind. That sounds like a reference to this wayward phase of ancient history."

"Thank you, Najdar, I should like to come back here often. I have heard there was an even older culture called Lemuria in the Pacific."

"Indeed, there was. I can take you there next time, if you'd like."

They walked out under the arches in deep silence, pondering the inscription about history repeating itself.

CHAPTER 26

Before the Great Karmic Board

"Well, Narayan, these last eight months of Earth time, while your mother has been preparing your body, have flown by and your day of birth draws nigh. It is time to again go before the Great Karmic Board as you did when you exited your last life."

"I always get a bit nervous before going before them. I think it is due to some unjust courts I have been taken before when on Earth," admitted Narayan.

"They are justice and mercy personified. They know your mission and they know your karma, and they will make sure you make the most of your life, both in terms of your personal, spiritual development and your mission in the world."

"I'm still a bit nervous. I now recall going before them at the beginning and end of each life. When I took my vows, I was so sure of myself, but when I descended into the density of the Earth, I so often forgot my promises. At the end of that life, they showed me the record of my missed opportunities and I became my own judge and jury."

"Don't worry. I will be there, as will several other masters who have shown interest in your soul and your work to come. Just go into deep meditation, and when you are ready, you will be escorted into their august presence."

As he opened his eyes, he was surprised at being before a large, alabaster building reminding him of the Parthenon of Ancient Greece. He remembered where to go, although an angel escort was there to bring him. They walked slowly up the white steps and a great calm filled his soul, knowing that complete justice and mercy would be administered in this court. As the golden doors swung open, Narayan felt a high vibration as he saw the seven Lords of Karma sitting on their thrones in a semicircle with a raised dais in the center where he would stand.

Behind them stood a number of masters. One was a tall man with a long beard, turban and flashing blue eyes. He recognized him as the master, El Morya. Another had a pointy beard with his blond hair combed back and violet eyes—this was Saint Germain. Baltar and Renatia stood behind him as he stood before these masters and cosmic beings. How they could minister to every soul after and before each lifetime was mind-boggling to him, but being masters of time and space, they managed it perfectly.

"Welcome, Narayan, Son of Light!" Beamed a master to the right wearing a blue robe and holding in his heart the divine plan for every soul. This one he recognized as the Great Divine Director. "We have watched your development over the centuries and are pleased that you have come to place your gifts upon the altar of humanity."

The lady master in the yellow robes next to him, looking very much as if she were the model used for the Statue of Liberty, spoke next. "Beloved Narayan, I am the Goddess of Liberty. As you know, your mission is two-fold: The first is to bring forth your own unique teaching to the world and thereby to fulfill your divine plan; the second is to balance at least 51% of your personal karma and by paying your debts to life, you may graduate Earth's schoolroom and join the liberated beings of Heaven, winning the victory of your ascension, moving on to higher levels of mastery, and serving all life from these inner levels."

Another beautiful woman, Ascended Lady Master Nada, wearing an ornate pink robe, unrolled a scroll. I have here the record given to me by the Keeper of the Scrolls. I find here a listing of all that has been a burden to your soul thus far. We would like to help you in laying out the best possible life that you can achieve. To this end, we are recommending that you balance as much karma as possible early in your life, so that later when you begin your mission, your personal load shall be much lighter."

The majestic Elohim to her side, Beloved Cyclopea, wearing white robes and an emerald crown, continued where she left off. "To counteract physical health problems that you will have to bravely deal with for the first eight years of your life, we will assign you to a practitioner of natural healing. Your mother shall contact this man soon after your birth. This practitioner will use entirely non-suppressive methods of healing so that you can have a fairly clean bill of health by the time you start your outer mission in early adulthood."

The exalted lady master, Pallas Athena, in a green outfit to Cyclopea's side, held a staff that looked like a spear. She looked deeply into Narayan's eyes and soul, saying, "Several masters have come forth to assist in sponsoring your lifestream and your mission." As she said this, the turbaned master stood forth and put a large, gleaming sapphire gem on the table before this divine woman.

El Morya spoke: "I offer this jewel that has been fused from my personal attainment. I have been careful of late in giving collateral on behalf of those who make vows before this assembly, for I have lost more than a few gems due to the forgetfulness of those who swore they wouldn't leave from their high and holy calling to bear truth to the Earth. However, I sense in Narayan a soul that will not fail. He has prepared well for this mission, and is deserving of my ray of protection around him that will deflect any encroachments by the dark forces against his service. Of course, I cannot guarantee his success, but I can promise I will do all in my power to assist him in completing his mission in service to the Light."

As Morya stepped back, the woman in the next chair stood up. She was Beloved Portia, Goddess of Justice, and she wore purple robes with a golden mantle. She stood for a while, looking at him and enfolding him in complete compassion. Then, she said, "We have had certain deliberations regarding your destiny, Narayan, and have come to a conclusion. As you now know, the soul named Sephira shall be your lifelong friend and cohort. But marriage and romance with her are not part of the equation. You will be guided to marry a woman who you have karma with and will be working all of this out with her for an extended period."

Portia paused and unrolled a scroll that was presented to her by one of the angels of records. "In your previous life, Narayan, this woman became pregnant by you and you promised to support her and the baby, but then you abandoned them both, leaving them to a life of poverty and struggle. And so, if you agree to balance this debt in this next life, your challenge will be to struggle financially to support them both and to remain faithful to her no matter what the temptation. She is a kind and gentle soul—a soul mate of yours—and after years of working out your karma together, sometimes with the help of therapists, you will find peace and resolution and will be a good support for each other. You will also accrue wonderful good karma by raising this child into responsible, conscious adulthood. He is another deserving soul who is an important part of your mandala."

The great master Saint Germain, with brilliant violet eyes, stepped forth and put his hand on Narayan's shoulder, saying, "Of course, there will be times of great happiness and pleasure in your marriage. In fact, the struggles in your family life will goad you to find solutions to many of your thorniest issues. Much of the answers you find will be the basis of the soul therapy work you will develop, which will become your life's work. Thus, every adversity you will experience contains the seed of an equal or greater benefit to be gained."

Finally, violet-robed Kuan Yin stood up and stepped out from behind the semi-circular table in front of them. She approached Narayan and opened her arms to him for an embrace. She then took his hands, and tuning into his heart, said, "Narayan, you are my dear friend, and you have been my student for centuries. I am a Goddess of compassion and mercy, and I live to serve. Now, you are coming into that same vibration, which you have access to from your great Causal Body of Light and your momentum on the violet ray. Your soul therapy will become a new psychology for those now entering into incarnation, and for their parents. We have waited a thousand years for the Earth to be ready for such accelerated wisdom. When a soul is connected to their God Presence, they are far less likely to make choices and karma of a negative nature. We are proud of who you are and the service you will render to mankind."

Kuan Yin then placed her hands upon his head. A violet flame sprung up all around him and completely consumed all anxiety he still maintained about his upcoming life. "When you are one with your soul, and your soul is one with God, then your vision of a new age will manifest."

Baltar then stepped forth and put both hands upon Narayan's shoulders. "Remember, peace in your feeling world is the key to manifesting your purpose. Great Karmic Lords, I have trained this soul to the best of my ability. I have helped him choose the right circumstances for his new life. I have given him the gift of the jewel of the heart so that he may always listen to the voice within. I want to personally thank you for granting his request for a new life. And by God's grace, this time he shall not fail!"

Narayan then spoke to all present: "I praise the One Almighty Living God for all that I am and all that I ever hope to be. As the master said, 'I of myself can do nothing.' So, I will allow that Light within to shine forth and do its perfect work through me. I thank you for your kind consideration, mercy and justice. I know I have said it before, but this time I really mean it. I will not fail. I will not let down my friends in Heaven and on Earth. We will win this victory for a Golden Age!"

As he left the room, he felt a renewed sense of purpose. He knew that what he had to do involved a team—other souls who have also trained themselves to be successful in their missions. He thought to himself: With all the light we have in our hearts, how can we fail? He had accomplished his preparation in Heaven, and now it was time for his entry into Earth. He realized that things had changed on Earth since his last sojourn.

He had done his research. There were more toxins in the environment, more distractions, more outer stimulation, more bombardment of the senses. Of course there had been so much good as well, immense progress in technology, in communication, in psychology, in medical research and in understanding how nature works.

With the little time left to him, when he was not floating in the womb, hearing the muffled sounds of his mother and her environment, feeling her feelings and tasting the flavors of her food in the amniotic fluid, he was cramming as if for a major exam.

He was shown some of the pivotal events being programmed into this next incarnation. When he's twelve and Jeff, the bully, demands his lunch money, he learned that the way he deals with this pivotal event will be the beginning of his mission. This is the same soul that Narayan stole money from in Germany almost two hundred years earlier. He would have to talk to his teacher about it and learn from her how to forgive, how to speak truth, and how to see the pain in the soul that causes people to act out in violence and aggression. This will inspire him to look for the deeper causes of people's actions and not to judge by outer appearances. When he converts Jeff to becoming his protector and friend, he will know that he has a gift.

When he is twenty-four and applying for a job, the receptionist would smile and say, "How may I help you?" and a glint of light would shine from the diamond on her pendant shaped like a musical note. That is going to be the sign that this young lady would become his future wife.

At the age of 40, when he is speaking before a large audience, he will notice a fourteen-year-old girl listening intently in the third row. That will make him understand that his mission is to focus on the youth, who are old enough to learn about the soul and to understand the eternality of their essence. They could prevent so many painful experiences by learning to listen to their intuition.

Because of the upbringing he will get from his father, he will always know that it is important to back up his beliefs and spiritual teaching with facts from science and research. He was shown that what is now called the paranormal will soon become part of mainstream science and general understanding. Sensitive cameras will be developed that will record invisible beings, as well as accurate images of the chakras and the aura. Healers will use these photos to detect and treat diseases before they become physical. More and more people will have their subtle senses functioning, with clairvoyance and clairaudience becoming commonplace. The majority of thinking people will accept reincarnation as a fact, along with the practical understanding of the law of karma. This will bring about a societal change where almost no one will be tempted to commit crimes or inflict suffering upon other forms of life, knowing for certain that their actions will come back to them for payment.

The mainstream will soon catch on to the devastating costs of industrial farming and food production, not only to health but also to the earth. All food will be grown organically or biodynamically, and harmful chemicals will gradually be eliminated from all of the products that people use, whether in farming, gardening, cosmetics, or cleaning products. Rural communities would begin to flourish again, and children will again be outside in nature for much of their day. When there is no more temptation for political leaders to use advanced technology for war, as they did on Atlantis, then free energy from what is now called Dark Matter would be deployed on a global scale, with unlimited energy and zero pollution.

Churches would gradually start espousing the more mystical paths that their founders had laid out, teaching their parishioners to have a more direct connection to the God within. There will be much more crossover between the religions. Christians may take up yoga, meditation, and Buddhist mantras for stilling the mind. Jews may dance while chanting Hindu *bhajans* as a joyous praise of the truth that there is but one God with many manifestations. Many churches will become Internet-based, where people can experience group prayer and meditation online, with teachings being enjoyed within one's own home.

There was so much hope he felt for Earth's future. And it was based upon the fact that he and millions of other souls have been trained well in the higher realms on how to make the Earth a better place. With the collapsing of many of the structures of the old order, a new culture would arise. These incoming children will know that they are not here for just themselves; they are here for the good of the whole. All for one and one for all is their mantra. They will exult in the simple pleasures of life, and their main passion will be helping others and helping nature to recover from centuries of abuse.

CHAPTER 27

A Heavenly Pet

Renatia called Narayan to take a break from his studies and meet a special guest. "Oh wow, a puppy. How cute!" and the little dog jumped into his arms and started licking his face. "Is this a gift for me?"

"This is to be a childhood companion to help you in the early years of your life. It will be a great comfort to you. It will teach you how love can be shared, and deep emotions exchanged, without the need for words or language."

"I will be so happy to have a little friend from Heaven with me on my sojourn to Earth. I'm sure we'll have so much fun and many adventures."

"I am afraid it will not all be fun and games. You see, as the Karmic Board mentioned, you will have some health issues as a child and these will be karmic in nature. Well, this being has volunteered to have her own health issues as she helps shoulder your burden. Then, at age 8, you shall be healed, but she will suffer greatly and then have to leave."

Suddenly the dog jumped down and started twirling and twirling, faster and faster, until it was just a blur of fur and light—and *poof!* There stood a living, breathing eight-inch, two-legged being that looked somewhere between an elf and a monkey, with a furry face.

"I know you!" exclaimed Narayan, "Is it you, Kaylee?"

"At your service once more, sir! It has been a while since I was your horse in Mongolia."

"And my elephant in India."

"And your camel in Arabia."

With that, she flew up in the air and kissed Narayan on the cheek. He then gave her a very gentle hug.

"Why a dog? I thought you liked large incarnations.

"Oh, I've done large, alright. I started out pretty early in my career as a brontosaurus—boy, was that hard to steer! But as a pet living with a human family, I can learn so much of what being human is about—compassion, tenderness, comfort. You see, as you are finishing up your rounds of being a human and are nearing the stage of becoming a master, thanks to my service to life and especially to you, I am about to earn a heart-flame and transition from the elemental kingdom to the human level of evolution. After thousands of years of development, starting out as a gnome, I will finally have earned the great opportunity of entering the path that leads to eternal life. One day, I too may have the glory of becoming an immortal master.

"I am amazed, Kaylee! I look forward to your being part of my family, but I don't want to burden you with my karma or illness. Please don't take that upon yourself! I would hate to see you, of all beings, suffer."

"As hard as it is, the cross of suffering is a path that most of us must walk at some point in our development. When we lay down our lives for our friends, as strange as it may seem, we make great strides on the path to eternal life."

At that, Kaylee spun on her toes in a miniature whirlwind, transforming back into a puppy. She gave Narayan a yip and lick and ran away.

"Oh, Renatia, thank you so much for that gift. We often think that humanity is all-important, but there are so many different life-forms that are all evolving on this planet as well."

"And they deserve your prayers for protection, as does their habitat. You'd be amazed at how much forest and rainforest has been cut down for very short-sighted development and commercialization. Many plants and animals are on the verge of extinction, after millions of years of careful and slow development."

"Well, as part of my teaching on the psychology of the soul, I plan on helping people connect to their spirits by communing with nature. I just hope there are enough of us descending that will insist that we put nature, beauty and preserving the planet above short-term profit."

CHAPTER 28

Visit with a Blue-Ray Master

Baltar informed Narayan that a great master would like a few words with him before he departs. "His is a retreat located in the etheric plane above Northern India, in the fastness of the snowcapped Himalayas. Don't be intimidated by his seeming gruffness. He demands toughness in his disciples because so much is resting on their shoulders—his love is equally large."

They went into meditation and he focused his attention upon the Himalayas. He felt rapid movement and heard a swishing sound until they arrived at a building reminiscent of the *Taj Mahal*. He was allowed in an entry room where a short, bearded, gnomish fellow seem irritated at his arrival.

"Do you have an invitation?"

"Yes. I believe I was invited."

"That's what they all say. You might have to wait a very long time. The master doesn't normally see the likes of you."

Narayan was feeling a bit heated and started to take offense. After all, he didn't ask for this visit in the first place. Maybe I should just leave, he thought to himself. But, he controlled himself. He sat on a cushion in meditation and just said, "I will wait."

A gong rang, and the door opened. There stool a tall, bearded figure with piercing blue eyes, wearing a turban.

"I see that you have survived my doorman. Thus, you may enter."

"You are the master who laid down your blue jewel for me at my Karmic Board meeting!"

"Indeed, you are correct. I am El Morya and this is my retreat at Darjeeling." They walked over a plush white carpet and sat facing each other before a roaring fire, which like his eyes, had a bluish tint. "That doorman has saved me so much energy—the ego-based and the curious go off in a huff, and I can focus on what is important."

"Baltar did not mention much about this meeting, but he was impressed that you sent for me. I had heard that you mostly deal with government leaders and world politics."

"My hand stirs many pots, but I champion the Will of God and will assist all who serve on the blue ray. I have been a king, a ruler, and a government official numerous times. They called me an honest politician and I have lost my head more than once for being so."

"In truth, I have no desire to be in government or any rulership position at all. You see, I am working on releasing a deeper teaching on the psychology of the soul."

"That is why you interest me. You see, I have had a string of setbacks recently. Some of my disciples, who pledged wholeheartedly to bring a Heavenly government to Earth have been so disgusted with the ugliness of politics and all its rampant corruption, that they declined in their vow to seek public office. Many are now running businesses and enjoying their lives. This is their choice to make, but they have left off from world service. We can see how the planet is suffering as a result."

"So, psychology is involved?"

"Exactly. You see, Narayan, the few lightbearers that finally get into the government are immediately set upon by temptation. Did you know that most politicians are taught how to take bribes without being detected, and shown how to open secret offshore accounts to keep their money hidden? Others, in weaker moments, may fall prey to an indiscretion where they are secretly taped doing things that their partners would not look favorably upon. Then, they are blackmailed into voting a certain way, or to pass a certain bill that will favor the elite. Oh, how I weep for their souls."

"This has to do with the psychology of the soul?"

"Ah, yes, your role. I would like to see your soul psychology work integrated into the school systems with various ages. I want people to have more integrity and honesty instilled at all levels. They must see that self-knowledge is the key to existence itself—especially the knowledge of their Higher Self."

"As in the saying: *To thine own Self be true!*"

"Exactly! So do your preparations, because I want the future leaders brought up with self-knowledge, both of their lower natures, in order to win their mastery in the lower planes, and of their Higher Self, so that when they assume positions of power and authority, they won't misuse the opportunity. Some of the other masters who sponsor souls in other areas of life have similar challenges. Why, I just recently spoke with a master who sponsors many artists, actors, and others that become influential in the entertainment industry. He is concerned that when these souls increase in fame, power and influence in society, it goes to their heads. Many of them will indulge in abuses of power involving sexual misconduct, hubris, greed, and excessive alcohol or drug addictions."

"And what kind of example is that to their devoted fans?"

"So, I see we are of one mind. I was right to place my trust in you, which is why I offered that gem—a portion of my Causal Body momentum on the blue ray in support of your embodiment. I will help to see that you are raised with integrity and protected by my flame so that you will grow into the fulfillment of your inner vows. And remember, if you falter or fail in your mission, it is I who will also pay the consequences."

"I will do my best, Master Morya. I thank you for your sponsorship and your trust."

"Indeed, Narayan, I thank you. Godspeed to you in the Will of God!"

CHAPTER 29

Blessing for Those Descending

N arayan had been summoned to a special blessing by a master who was to address the souls that were about to embody from these particular schools of light within the next month. About eight thousand souls gathered in a large amphitheater. A man dressed in white robes stood at the podium and looked around the room.

The Master began, "I am known as the Maha Chohan. I convey the flame of the Holy Spirit, which is the white light, the merging of the seven rays—the seven paths to personal Christhood. Each of you has specialized in the mastery of one ray, but you all have accumulated talents and momentum on all of the rays. You have prepared long and hard for your upcoming embodiments on Earth. I know you will remain true to the flame of the Presence upon the altar of your hearts. I will now pour out a blessing upon you as I sing this inspired poem to your souls. This will instill light within you that contains secret codes within all the rays of God. This will assist you to never forget the reason for your descent."

He raised his palms in blessings and a tangible waterfall of power rained down upon the audience in liquid rainbow rays of light, as his voice rang out: "In the name and by the power of your own Mighty God Presence, I now bless and release each of you upon your soul journey." With dramatic solemnity, the Maha Chohan recited these verses:

> *In the soul there dwells a Light*
> *that only God can see—*
> *A pattern of perfection there,*
> *a desire to be free.*

In the realms of glory,
  before the soul takes birth,
There is only joy and victory—
  a feeling of self-worth.
A planning and preparing,
  a hope for things to come—
A wishing and a hoping
  that God's pure Will be done!

In the deepest part of self,
  beyond all time and space,
Is stored a vault of love—
  precipitated grace.
The jewels of past good works,
  the wind within the sail,
Shall guide the spirit onward
  beyond the human veil.
I know that God is in me
  as I shall soon depart.
This knowing and belonging
  remains with me a part.
I will soon be in duality,
  where things seem to oppose,
Where the sharp and painful thorn
  supports the lovely rose.

They say that on the Earth
  that there can be some pain,
But in the end, it's worth it,
  for experience we gain.
From all the growth and learning
  we cannot gain above,
We understand at last
  it's all about the Love.
We must forgive our enemies
  and those we just can't stand.
We see those stuck in suffering

and extend a helping hand.
They say at the end of life,
* it all went in a flash—*
That only what you gave away
* in Heaven is your 'cash.'*
For millionaires who hoarded all,
* now buried with the shovel,*
Are found within a lower plane
* dwelling in a hovel.*

And those who dwelt in lack
* but with their little given,*
Have a mansion in the sky—
* a little piece of Heaven.*

A guarantee is never given
* to those who must descend.*
On the inner light alone,
* on that they must depend.*
Teachers, parents, pundits
* all try to point the way.*
Will you follow their guidance?
* Only you can truly say.*

Will they teach you to be silent,
* to turn off all that noise?*
To be still and listen,
* to hear the inner voice?*
The conscience they do call it,
* the Mind of God within.*
If you only listen to it
* the game of life you'll win.*

We understand your hesitance
* to enter Earth right now.*
With so many distractions,
* How will you keep your vow?*

But Earth, she cries for healing—
  resolution of her pain.
Will you go help her now
  in God's most Holy Name?

You will never be alone—
  you're part of a vast team.
All of Heaven's with you
  though alone you'll sometimes seem.
We demand the Victory
  that all might know self-worth!
As long as one soul's lost
  upon this sphere of Earth,
We'll send the spirits hence,
  those students of the Light,
 Who long have been preparing
  to take the downward flight.

We see a time of glory
  where everyone's a sage
The dawning of Aquarius—
  a blessed Golden Age.
Kindness, love and charity,
  the opening of the heart—
The culture enjoyed in Heaven
  on this planet will now start.

So parents, guides and teachers
  Please heal all of your rifts.
So that these souls descending
  may unfold all of their gifts.
As the rainbow in the sky
  blesses all in rays of seven,
Father, thy Will be done on Earth
  as it is in Heaven!

For the next few minutes, there was an awesome silence as all absorbed this light and message into their souls. There was nothing more to say, as one-by-one, they started filing out of the large chamber. Many looked deeply into the eyes of each other, placing their hands in prayer position at their hearts, and bowing to the light within each other. They sent silent prayers that they, too, would remember their missions and embody the fulfillment of the highest potential of their soul.

~ ~ ~ *EPILOGUE* ~ ~ ~

*A*lthough it took a tremendous amount of energy, Renatia, the guide who was helping Baltar train his pupil, was able to impress upon Narayan's parents the need to enlist the assistance of a midwife, Bessie, for the latter part of the pregnancy and birth. When Jennifer's iron showed to be too low, the only thing that really helped was eating liver. She could touch the belly without using ultrasound, which she felt stressed the baby, and could tell its exact position.

Bessie said the baby was breach and that Jennifer should request the baby to turn its head downward. She employed an ancient Chinese medicine technique to turn the baby. She heated up what looked like a long cigar, which was made of the herb mugwort, called moxa. She pecked the moxa stick back and forth, heating up an acupuncture point on the outside corner of the mother's pinky toenail. She then placed a large quartz crystal with its point downward on Jennifer's belly. Within ten minutes, a large bump moved down the front of her belly. The baby had assumed the correct position for delivery.

Stuart was so impressed with the result that he asked the midwife if he would benefit from acupuncture himself. She took some time feeling the twelve pulses of his radial artery of his wrists. She said that the quality of the pulses gave her information about the state of health of his organs. She examined his tongue and said something about the whitish coating, indicating some dampness in his spleen and the teeth marks around the edges of the tongue denoting a chi deficiency. She guessed correctly that he had weak digestion and low energy levels.

Bessie was an acupuncturist first, with a secondary interest in pregnancy. Later on, she had taken the training to become a midwife as well. Although she didn't treat too many men, she sometimes would treat the husbands to help them chill out, which helped the *birth process and the energy of the whole family.*

She cleaned areas of his body with an alcohol pad and inserted very thin stainless-steel needles into acupuncture points below his knees, on the inside of his ankles, near his wrist, and below his navel. He was amazed that he felt no pain at all, and only felt a little electrical zing when she twirled the needles in the inside of his wrists. She explained that energy was circulating throughout his body in meridians (vital-energy pathways) below the skin, which are connected to the major organs. When the energy circulation was balanced, she felt his pulses again and told him that the energy flow in his organs was improved.

She promised to help him further, and said that building Jennifer's energy after the delivery would be important as well, not only with acupuncture, but also with Chinese herbs and special blood-building soups. They agreed that because of Jennifer's age, a hospital birth would be best, but that they would try to utilize the medical staff only as a last resort if there were problems.

After Jennifer's water had broken at home, Bessie, the midwife, instructed both parents to meet her in the birthing room at the hospital. Stuart drove up to 90 miles an hour on the highway to the hospital.

Stuart tried to help Jennifer with the breathing exercises they had learned, but Jennifer didn't want to hear it. Since they didn't want to do an epidural anesthetic, they tried electro-acupuncture for the pain, and it was surprisingly successful. After three hours of gradually increasing contractions, she was fully dilated.

When they hooked up the fetal monitors, they saw a problem. Whenever Jennifer would give a big push, her heartbeat would slow down significantly. The obstetrician on call was concerned, and when Bessie reached in, she could feel that the umbilical cord was wrapped around the baby's neck. The doctor felt a Caesarian section was in order, especially as Jennifer was exhausted from all the pushing.

Bessie looked deep into Jennifer's eyes and said firmly, "We can do this without a C-section!" *Narayan felt like he was being strangled. He was turning blue. Then an image flashed into his mind. He was at a gallows. The noose was put around his neck and the bottom dropped out. He thought: Oh, not again, not with all my planning. How unjust!*

Then he saw another vision. He was a judge, he took his gavel, and pointed at the suspect and declared, "Death by hanging!" Suddenly, he felt a strong hand push him backwards, which slipped the cord off his throat. He felt oxygen flowing into his brain again. There was intense pressure on his head and after a short time, there was a release.

In his inner vision, he saw the Maha Chohan breathe the breath of the Holy Spirit into his mouth. Then it came—his first breath—and a high-pitched cry emitted from his tiny lungs. "It's another boy!" *Bessie declared as she put the baby to his mother's breast, not bothering to first wipe him off, much to the chagrin of the nurses. She waited for the cord to stop pulsing and let Stuart have the honor of cutting the cord himself. After blood sprayed into his glasses, he wept tears of joy.*

Narayan sensed such a great thirst, as if he was a desert that was yearning for the rain. He felt himself being brought up to the heart of his mother. Then, something touched his lips and he instinctively latched on the breast. Oh, what sweet bliss he felt as that warm heavenly liquid quenched that awful thirst. He had finally made it. He felt at peace.

Eight children were born in the hospital that day, each one having a role to play in the great mission of the salvation of Earth. Multiplied by the millions of children descending, it becomes clear that the future of Earth is bright. We should all have great hope.

~~~ *RECOMMENDED READING* ~~~

The following authors and books have been influential in my decades of research into the mystical and esoteric teachings of East and West, which form the background for the stories and concepts depicted in this book. I recommend them for further study.   —*Warren King*

A Dweller on Two Planets
    Baumgardt Publishing Company, 1905
    Phylos the Thibetan, through Frederick S. Oliver

At the Feet of the Master, The Theosophical Society, 1910
    Jiddu Krishnamurti

Autobiography of a Yogi, Self-Realization Fellowship, 1946
    Paramahansa Yogananda

Brother of the Third Degree, Garver Communications, 1984
    Will L. Garver

Climb the Highest Mountain, The Summit Lighthouse, 1972
    Mark and Elizabeth Prophet

Life and Teaching of the Masters of the Far East (Vol. 1–5)
    1924, DeVorss & Co, 1964
    Baird T. Spalding

Saint Germain Series, Saint Germain Press
    Unveiled Mysteries, Vol. 1, 1934
    The Magic Presence, Vol. 2, 1935
    The "I AM" Discourses, Vol. 3, 1935
        Godfre Ray King

Studies of the Human Aura, The Summit Lighthouse, 1975
  Mark Prophet

The Agni Yoga Series
  17 Titles, Agni Yoga Society, 1923–1941
  Nicholas and Helena Roerich

The Aquarian Gospel of Jesus the Christ:
The Philosophic and Practical Basis of the Religion of the
Aquarian Age of the World and of the Church Universal
  E. S. Dowling, 1908
  Levi H. Dowling

The Bridge to Freedom Dispensation
  Over 70 Titles, Ascended Master Teaching Foundation,
  1952–1961
  Geraldine Innocente

The Masters and the Path, The Theosophical Society, 1925
  Charles W. Leadbeater

The Masters and Their Retreats, The Summit Lighthouse,
  2003, Mark Prophet and Elizabeth Clare Prophet

Made in the USA
Columbia, SC
25 June 2018